The Ten Rule

CW00867489

THREE CHILDREN KILLED IN TRAGIC ACCIDENT

Report by
Laura Martin

YESTERDAY a mother and kids were squashed out of existence when a lorry overturned on their car. "It was freaky", said a by-stander. "The lorry tipped right over when it

Story: Zella Compton

Art: Jess Swainson

MOGZILLA

The Ten Rules of Skimming

First published by Mogzilla in 2012.

ISBN: 9781906132262

Story & concept copyright © 2011 Zella Compton
Artwork copyright © Jess Swainson
Cover copyright © Mogzilla 2011

Printed in the UK

The right of Zella Compton to be identified as the author of this work has been asserted in accordance with the Copyright, Designs and Patent Act 1998. This book is sold subject to the condition that it shall not, by way of trade or otherwise, be lent, resold, hired out, or otherwise circulated without the publisher's prior consent in any form of binding or cover other than that in which it is published and without a similar condition including this condition being imposed on the subsequent publisher.

www.mogzilla.co.uk/skimming

Zella would like to thank the following people:
Garnett, Griffin, Hebe and Orla. Jess, all the Baldocks, Jim (RIP), Maire, Jennie, Siobhan, Jo and Mogzilla.

Jess would like to thank the following people:
Robin, Zella, Paul, Toby, Mum, Dad, Gran, Maxine, Laura, Spanner, Peter and Janet.

Chapter one

IT WAS A SIMPLE QUESTION.

"I need all the details," the Questioner said. "The only way I can help you is if you tell me everything."

Adam looked at the older man sat opposite him.

He'd followed him into the basement of the hospital. The place had endless corridors with hundreds of sweaty feet squelching up and down in sandals, rising and falling, keeping time with the births and deaths. Now Adam was regretting his decision. He was going to be stuck here for hours and there was no guarantee that this man could save him from the fury of the Board and the consequences of his actions.

"Where shall I begin?" Adam asked.

"At the start. How did you discover you could skim?"

"It started in this hospital, a ward somewhere above here."

Adam smiled at his Questioner, hoping he could remember all the details. He relaxed back into his chair and spoke so softly that the Questioner moved the old fashioned Dictaphone further forward and started taping their conversation.

"It happened like this…"

Adam put his hands behind his head and began his story.

How long should a dutiful grandson visit an unconscious relative for? Was saying 'hello' enough? Adam ran his hand through his hair. It was dark and tangled like his grandfather's. Deciding that ten minutes more visiting would do, he found a chair, sat down and closed his eyes. Moments later, he was asleep but standing up and looking around in confusion.

In the distance at the foot of a hill, a kid – about his age – was running desperately up the slope, trying to get to the farmhouse. The wind was pushing him backwards and even from here, Adam could see that he was sweating furiously.

"Hey!" Adam called and raised his hand but the boy was intently focused on the farmhouse and the wind carried Adam's greeting away.

The farmhouse door opened and a stout figure appeared: a woman in a billowing skirt with a pinny on the front, her shirt sleeves rolled up to her elbows.

She looked at the running boy and raised her arms. Silver glinted briefly between her hands in a shaft of light through the black clouds, and then it came, the peel of the bell she was holding. It was one of the sweetest sounds Adam had ever heard: clear, crisp, direct. The boy fell defeated, his hands deep in mud.

Adam jolted upright and found himself back in the ward. He sat perfectly still, trying to keep his head fresh.

He'd been so cold, but now the heat was creeping through him, spreading upwards through his body, toes, knees, into arms, down to hands. Hands that lay encased in his grandfather's. Adam pulled away.

The Questioner retreated into his chair, his face hidden in the gloom from the single bulb. A fraction of a second passed. He placed his hands on the coffee table, next to the Dictaphone, its red light blinking solemnly. He moved it an inch one way, and then back, as if practising controlling his hands, before his fingers, yellow from nicotine, tapped its shiny black case.

"You shouldn't smoke," said Adam.

"I don't," the Questioner replied. He smiled widely, revealing a matching set of yellowing teeth.

"It's quite a power to skim into peoples' minds."

"I didn't know what it was then," Adam said, "so I did some research."

Chapter two

SHE WAS WEARING HER WHITE-STRIPED BAKING APRON. Flour highlighted her hair where she'd absent-mindedly pushed it out of her face.

"You sound too much like your father Adam."

His mother turned her back to build her cake, shoulders working determinedly. She said: "Try to be a bit more like your sister. She knows how important family is to me."

Her spoon banged loudly against the bowl's side.

"Tell me about when grandad was a boy," said Adam.

She loved to talk about family. It was the only way that she could be won round in times of stress.

"I'm busy. Cakes don't make themselves Adam."

"I know. You do and they're great."

This was a lie. Adam was happy to tell it and his mother to hear it. She stirred the mixture furiously as if she wanted her family to be able to taste her anxiety.

"Haven't you got a school project to finish?" she asked.

"I did it at the start of the holiday," Adam lied. "Go on mum, this'll be our 'quality' time for the year."

Adam listened as his mother put her cake into the oven and talked about her family history. The conversation took circular routes with Adam leading her back through time to where he wanted to be. Finally they got there.

"Of course when your grandfather was a boy he didn't get to slope off for the afternoon. Any time he had was spent on the farm, feeding the animals, watering, planting trees, working."

Adam bit his tongue. He wished she'd stop trying to prove how lazy he was! All he wanted was a description of that farmhouse. Quite how this had happened was beyond him. He needed to snap her out of it, but it was too late. She'd got into one of her usual 'states', ending her rant with: "He had no time to himself – not like you."

Adam walked slowly through the kitchen door trying to arrange his shoulders in a hurt fashion. The crisp smell of burning sultanas pricked his nose. A voice called after him:

"Some of your grandad's stuff is in the attic."

Adam stopped short, his foot suspended in mid-air.

"Thanks mum," he said and meant it.

Forty minutes, thirteen boxes, two lungs full of dust and one suitcase later Adam found what he was looking for.

The case was full of old photographs of Adam's grandad. There was one of him as a teenager glaring sulkily at the lens. In another he'd grown older and wiser and he stood with his mother in front of a farmhouse.

Adam leant towards the light that came weakly through the attic hatch. His heart beat quickly. It had to be the same house! Its 'schooner' weather vane was unique. This was the house that

11

the boy – who was surely his grandfather – had been running towards, but Adam was sure he hadn't seen these pictures before. So how could he have imagined it so well at the hospital?

At the bottom of the suitcase a packet lay swaddled in blue cloth. Adam peeled away the wrapping to reveal a hand bell.

Its handle rose gracefully and held the gentle imprint of many hands. Disappointingly Adam couldn't tell if it was the same one from his experience.

It was time to face it. He'd had an odd moment, a bizarre connection with his grandad and it was one of those things. Worrying about it was pointless. The truth of it was he was killing time putting off doing his summer project.

Adam stumbled to his feet. He put his hand down to steady himself but knocked into the bell. It rolled sedately towards the edge of the hatch, paused as if to say 'farewell' and dropped.

Marion's scream from below sliced the house in two.

Adam peered down. Marion's bright blue eyes, mirrors of his own, looked up inquisitively. Then she was gone along the hallway, bell in hand. Its sweet peel rang through the house.

"You found it," his mother called, but Adam didn't reply. He slumped onto the attic's edge, head in hands, attempting to get his brain around the impossible. It was one thing to dream up his grandfather's past, but it was quite another to hear it as well.

The Questioner smiled benignly.

"But you must have skimmed them?" he asked.

"Would you like to know your mother's every thought? She wishes it was me that disappeared instead of my sister."

"Fair enough," said the Questioner, leaning back on his chair. "So you tried to find Marion?"

"I couldn't. I was barred. Locked inside my own head. D'you want to hear about that now, or shall I continue in order?"

The Questioner smiled again. "In order," he said.

Chapter three

THERE WERE TOO MANY 'IFS' IN ADAM'S LIFE. If he'd completed his project, he wouldn't have got into trouble at school. The head wouldn't have rung his mum. He wouldn't have been grounded.

Adam lay on his bed and looked at his school bag. The project could wait, he had to think about what was happening.

The bell was real enough. Marion had squirreled it away. The pictures were real too. Had he seen into his grandad's past? He decided it must have been a vivid dream and ignored the voice that kept reminding him how cold he'd felt. Feeling freezing didn't fit the 'dream' theory. He didn't know what to think.

The late afternoon sun streamed through the window. Outside Marion was shouting nonsense at her friends. They were playing a game that involved numbers and hopping. He tried to block out the noise and thought about the anger management techniques his mum had been watching on day-time TV. In order to relax, they said you had to follow the pulse running from your brain through your body.

Adam tried to mould his body into his duvet. Spiderman! He must speak to his mum about that. He was 13 now, not a kid!

"Seven hops," Marion shrieked in the garden.

His heartbeat drummed out its rhythm. Adam's mind chased each beat around his body, through his torso, down his arms, up his legs, across his skin. He was slowing down, shutting out the noise from outside until all that filled his head was a steady beat echoing around the room. Then he felt something in his blood.

The bubbles were everywhere, spilling from his blood into every part of him, churning relentlessly until suddenly, there was blackness and he was no longer in his bedroom. Adam didn't recognise the place where he was standing. An infinite space stretched around him and he was multiplying to fill it. There was him, then him from the moment before, and him when he cried that day last September, and when he blew out the candles on his seventh birthday, and him giggling at the TV. Every moment he'd ever lived stretched as far as he could see, one of him for every second of his thirteen year existence.

Golden bubbles followed the smallest flick of his fingers. Adam was fascinated by the effect it created in this black space. He began to run – bubbles streaming out behind him – picking up speed, swirling, circling into the void.

Adam raised an arm and watched golden bubbles shoot from his fingertips, as all the other Adam's did the same in perfect synchronicity. Then he realised they were not copies. They were him. He felt their thoughts, breathed their air. He was a single person made up of millions of seconds in time. It was the most beautiful feeling.

All of the Adams were fascinated with the way that he moved and the effect it created in this black space.

He jumped and arched his spine, turning somersaults backwards. All of him in perfect synchronization, spiralling upwards, flipping down, no boundaries.

Adam's bodies did whatever his mind suggested, filling him with an immense sense of power.

The Questioner rubbed his hands together and produced a tube of hand cream.

"You want some?" he asked. One of his fingernails was so long it curled over on itself. He pushed the Dictaphone towards

Adam, palms upturned, pools of hand cream gleaming.

"How did you channel yourself?" the Questioner asked.

"I held hands with all the me's."

Adam was nervous. The threat of being permanently locked down hung around his neck. How could he explain this 'illegal' process that he'd discovered by accident? It came so naturally to him.

"I wanted to back flip – all of us at the same time. The circle was so massive I couldn't see the other side. My heart beat surfed through us, connecting us. Then we, I, back flipped. As we came back up into one place, we joined together into one body. It was explosive, gold everywhere, bubbles bursting, energy so thick, I was about to implode and explode unless I went somewhere. I had no choice but to leap into the blackness. I went faster and on and on until I shot into someone else's head."

"Whose?" the Questioner asked.

Chapter four

ADAM GLANCED AROUND NERVOUSLY. His bubbles were the only light in this thick edgy darkness. Marion's voice in the distance was still dictating to her friends. He knew he shouldn't be where he was, there was something not quite right. He was breathing quickly, a swell of excitement running through him.

The darkness disappeared as if a light had been switched on, burningly bright. He blinked furiously. And then the light was gone, as if a curtain had been drawn across a window.

'Did they see me? Be quick,' someone thought, straight into Adam's brain. 'Front door: locked and bolted. Safe.'

Adam looked in wonder as the hands ransacked everything in their path, grabbing valuables and stuffing them into pockets.

The house was vaguely familiar, but there was no time to place the memory – he was moving again. Upstairs, three bedrooms spilled off the landing. The person he was in seemed to know where they were going. He entered the master bedroom and looked around. He made directly to a jewellery box, spilled its contents out onto a dressing table and pocketed a diamond necklace and some rings. He opened drawers and rifled through them finding passports and foreign money. Satisfied with his pickings, he crashed back downstairs, keeping up a running commentary as he went.

'Sitting room: fireplace, sofas, CDs, laptop (bagged), candlesticks (scooped). TV, stereo: poor quality, remotes (pocketed).'

Marion screamed outside: "Three's a jump."

'Phone, pens, glass star ornament bagged.'

A doorbell buzzing screeched into Adam's head, pulling him back to his own body instantly, bubbles ripping at his seams.

He scrambled to his feet in his bedroom, and stumbled, dizzy, as if he'd just stepped off the fastest waltzer a fairground could offer. He made his way downstairs, holding onto the banisters for support. The doorbell buzzed again.

Adam stood stock-still. Break in? Now he knew where he recognised the house he'd been in, it was the neighbour's place. He'd been burgling next door.

"Wait!" Adam spluttered. The neighbour didn't stop. He pushed through the house, out into Adam's garden and eyed the fence.

Marion and her friends gathered around curiously.

"I'm locked out," the neighbour explained to Marion as he tried to scale the fence to get back to his own property.

"Your wife's home," Marion said, "I saw the curtains move."

"She is not!" said the neighbour, puffing out each word as he scrambled to find foot holes in the fence.

"I saw someone in there," Marion said defiantly.

"You go Adam," said the neighbour. "You're fitter than me."

Adam was over the fence in seconds, jumping down into the garden. He forced himself to look up at the windows.

He had just been inside a burglar's head in real time. The burglar must have locked himself in the house so he wouldn't get disturbed. Did he know that Adam was outside?

"Did mum buy you a mobile?" called Marion. "That's not fair! I'm more at risk than you. I'm a girl."

The back door sprang open and the burglar raced across the lawn. Adam skirted around him.

"Get him," yelled the neighbour excitedly as Marion and her friends chanted: 'Go Adam! Go Adam!'

The burglar turned, frantically looking for a route out.

The neighbour's precious possessions flew out of the burglar's bag and fell from his pockets as he flailed wildly around the garden. Seeing that there was no easy way to escape, the burglar stood still and dropped the bag.

"And the rest," said Adam.

"That's it mate," said the burglar, putting his palms up.

"The rings," Adam hissed. "The diamond necklace?"

The burglar stood uncertainly. "Whatever," he muttered emptying his pockets.

Adam knelt down to pick up the jewellery where it had scattered across the grass. Shouting insults, the burglar sprinted off through the house and out of the front door leaving the neighbour howling in frustration.

The Questioner wheezed deeply and coughed into his hands.

"Who did you skim next in your quest to become a super-hero?"

Adam felt uncomfortable. Being a crime-fighter had only appealed to him for about five minutes.

"Or did you think about going the other way? To become a villain? That's closer to what really happened isn't it?"

"I never wanted to . . ." Adam paused.

He nearly said: "kill a man." But that would have been a confession. So instead he said:

"It was a couple of days before I skimmed again..."

Chapter five

ADAM LAY ON HIS BED WITH HIS HANDS BEHIND HIS HEAD AND LET THE GOLDEN LIGHT TAKE CONTROL.

This time he expected the moment, relaxed into it and waited for it to clear, keenly searching for some clue as to who he was in. But all was blank.

Adam's host was filled with nothingness. No energy, or calm, just emptiness. Then the darkness cleared. The person he was in was sitting in an armchair dropping off to sleep. One eye closed, a slight snore and jolt, both eyes open, then shut.

"Dad," Marion yelled, and grabbed his arm.

'Shouldn't she be in bed by now?' Adam's father thought.

Adam sprung backwards in shock to his own body. He leant over the side of his bed and threw up.

Adam shifted uncomfortably.

"At the time, I was still learning. I didn't realise I had to skim between people to get to wherever I wanted, it's one of the rules."

The man made a note on a shabby piece of paper.

"Are they the Board's rules?"

'No. They're my rules, well, more like instructions."

"What do you mean 'instructions'? Like: 'Stand on one leg."

"They're hard to explain."

"Try me. I'm not stupid. Why don't you start by defining 'skimming' for me?"

"It's like bouncing a stone across water, but instead I move across peoples' minds.'

"It means," Adam began, "that you have to know where you are starting from, where exactly you are. You have to start 'close to shore' and skim out from there, from head to head. If you go too far on the first skim, you'll probably just sink. With no energy to move along, there's no way back."

"Go on," said the Questioner nodding sagely.

"The second and third rules are obvious. Start in the shallows, and know your way back. Most people use connectors to get back, but I didn't know that at the start."

"You were lucky to stay alive," the Questioner said with a tinge of admiration.

"I'm a fast learner. The Board will be furious with me for telling you this."

27

"The Board and I have a unique relationship. I told you, there's nothing to worry about. I'll make sure they don't lock you down again. How did lockdown feel by the way?"

Adam shifted in his chair. Awakening from lockdown was a vivid memory, one that he hated reliving.

"Spod warned me but I didn't believe her, I thought she was crazy."

"Oh yes," smiled the Questioner. "Spod. I was wondering when we'd come to her part in this."

TELL ME ABOUT SPOD...

Chapter six

AT SCHOOL, ADAM DIDN'T OFFEND OR EXCITE ANYONE. He was a kid with no allegiances, who gets invited to enough parties, who gets average grades, who both cool and nerdy kids talk to when there's no one else around. It had been like this since he was six. The world hadn't bothered him and he didn't bother it back. He was, in essence, uninspiring.

But times had changed. Now he had a stalker: Spod.

At the age of six, Jenny-Ray Harris as she was actually christened, bore an unfortunate similarity to a potato and had been named 'Spud.' Although she'd battled against the nickname, she'd lost the war and settled for being known as 'Spod.' By the time she became a senior, many students didn't have a clue who Jenny-Ray was, but they all knew Spod.

And for some reason that Adam didn't understand, she was now following him around like a love-sick puppy. Talking of dogs, a local stray was stalking him as well. The dog waited for him every morning and followed him around the school grounds. It walked him home and sat outside his front door. It took no notice of the cats that also followed him. Or the other dogs, or the birds that stopped chattering as he passed.

"Turn it off," Spod hissed.

"Eh?" said Adam, swatting butterflies off his shoulders.

"There's animals following you two by two – you look like Noah," she said. "Turn it off now!"

Adam ignored her and strode across the concrete playground, where the doors were barred by Mr Jenkins, the caretaker.

"What've you done? Stuffed your pockets with dog food?"

"No," said Adam, trying to dodge the muddy paws.

"You're glowing," hissed Spod. "Control yourself."

"Let me in Sir!" Adam pleaded.

Mr Jenkins' arms moved as if unfolding, then his resolve strengthened.

"Get rid of those animals first," he said, "I'm not spending my day up to my ears in dog muck."

"Nice image Sir!" said Spod. She turned to Adam. "You know what to do, turn it off," she whispered.

"What are talking about?" snapped Adam.

"Turn what off?" asked Jenkins suspiciously. "Have you got one of those whistles that gets animals to follow you?"

"I haven't got anything," said Adam testily.

"He's got a disease," said Spod unhelpfully. "Very rare and super contagious. It was on telly last night. Didn't you see it Sir? It was brilliant."

"You'd better go home." Mr Jenkins poked a finger in Adam's direction. "I'll tell the office . . ."

"Close contact is the thing that transmits it," said Spod. "They put you in quarantine..."

"And you'd better get to your class girl. Off you go!"

Jenkins slammed the door on them.

"I honestly have no idea what you're talking about," said Adam. "Do you think I want this?"

He glanced down and kicked viciously at a dog sniffing around his legs.

"Stop doing that!" Spod yelled in horror. "That poor dog can't help it."

"If you don't mind, I have a day to fill," said Adam. He wanted to stomp off but first he had to step over a kitten which was smooching around his legs.

Spod tried to restrain it. It wanted to be as close to Adam as it could get.

"You're like the Pied Piper of Pets," she laughed.

She followed along behind him through the gates and up the pathway behind the school. It was lined with hedges leading to wide fields. Litter marked smaller paths that wormed off it, through the long grass.

Adam ignored Spod and pulled his rucksack higher up his back. He was trying to figure out what he should turn off. The pathway wouldn't last forever, he needed a solution before he had to make his way across the main road with an army of crazy animals at his heels.

If he could pin down when all these creatures had became so besotted with him, maybe he could work it out.

The day after Adam visited his grandfather in hospital, the dog had appeared in the playground. It hadn't taken any notice of him. He'd watched from the cafeteria as it tore between the kids sitting in the playground searching for food. Then, there was been nothing for a few days. No dog, no cats, no unusual animal related incidents. On the Tuesday, the dog had appeared again and made straight for him. That had been the day of the burglary – when he'd discovered his new ability.

"That's it," he yelled excitedly, startling the dog at his heels. "That's when I started bubbling!"

"I know you're a skimmer," said Spod firmly. "What's more, your connector is useless. Are they a student?" she asked. "You're leaking energy all over the place."

Adam stopped walking.

"Can you help me?" he said.

"Who is your connector?" asked Spod. "What if the Board find out?"

"Stop talking gibberish and tell me how to get rid of these animals," Adam snapped.

"You're in control. Rein in the 'bubbles'. It's the energy they're after."

"What do you mean?" Adam hissed.

"Who's connecting you?" demanded Spod. She looked at Adam with concern. "You don't have a connector, do you?"

She put her hand up to Adam's face as it dawned on her.

"Help me! Please?" This was as close to begging as Adam had ever come.

Adam looked up and down the path, there was no one there to witness his humiliation, so he did as he was told. Spod's hands touched either side of his face, before she pushed them gently into his hair, and her fingers met around the back of his crown.

"I'm here," she whispered, "let me in."

Her forehead touched his and then Spod entered his mind.

They were in Adam's dark plain, except this time she was there and while his millions of selves stretched for infinity, Spod's stretched further. Each of the Spod's was connected to each of the Adam's with a silvery light.

The millions of Spods took up position around the millions of Adams, pulling him and his bubbles together. The bubbles squirmed furiously in the space between them.

"Hold them with your mind," she whispered.

Adam breathed deeply, pulling his energy back, turning on the spot, feeling each of his copies meld back into him. Squeezed by Spod, he became one person on the plain for the first time.

"We're done. That's enough – let's go back,' said Spod.

But Adam couldn't open his eyes. Her hands were in his hair, her head against his. If he broke the spell, the warm darkness would disappear.

And then she brushed his lips with hers, and said:

"Wake up."

"What was that about?" Adam said wiping his mouth.

Spod ignored him and looked at the animals departing.

"They're going!" said Adam, with relief.

"They've nothing to stay for now your bubbles are under control."

"Why is it called skimming anyway?"

"You skim between hosts, across the top of minds," Spod said. Her forehead crinkled in puzzlement. "You should know this. Haven't you been taught anything?"

Then she stared at him with concern. Her face paled.

"You seriously don't have anything to do with the Board do you?" she gasped. "Which means you're not registered. I shouldn't be helping you!"

"I have no idea what you're on about," Adam said.

"How did you learn about this?" asked Spod angrily.

"I taught myself. What's with all the questions?"

"You're a Board spy! You're setting me up!" she yelled.

"I'm not a spy," Adam shouted.

She was frightening him now.

"And you're a liar," Spod said. "It's impossible to teach yourself. How long have the Board been after me? Is this a test? I was so close to my license and now you've ruined everything."

She turned her back on him and set off down the path.

"Wait! I don't know what you are talking about," Adam said miserably to her back. "Spod?" he called. "Don't go."

She turned to face him, her face was red and blotchy. She wiped her nose fiercely on her sleeve.

"They'll lock me down tonight: 'For my own good'. I'll be stuck, like the rest of the idiots in this town, trapped in my head with no escape. Thanks." She snorted back her tears. "And goodbye."

"I'm telling the truth," said Adam.

Spod rounded on him.

"Then you're in trouble as well," she said.

The next morning, Spod appeared at Adam's front door.

"I'm sorry, okay?," Spod hung her head guiltily. "You're not a spy. Unless this is a huge double cross and I'm going to be locked down later."

"Stop it will you?" said Adam. His toes were blue. He regretted the fact he'd decided his slippers were uncool and come out in bare feet. Who was he trying to impress, Spod?

"I'll make it up to you. Come round to my house after school." she said firmly. "I'll explain some skimming basics."

"Will you go mad at me again?" asked Adam.

"I promise to be nicer," Spod said. Adam snorted.

"Whatever," he muttered and went back inside.

"Was that your friend Jenny?" asked Adam's mum. She was stood in the hallway dusting cobwebs from picture frames with his dad's favourite tie. Adam ignored her and went back to bed.

Chapter seven

SPOD TOOK HER ROLE AS ADAM'S INSTRUCTOR SERIOUSLY. By the time he arrived she'd built a lectern on her desk from a pile of shoeboxes. Ribbons hung from Spod's ceiling in a mad variety of colours, and they glistened with shiny ornaments hung on the ends. Her curtains were made of strips of gauze, held on a woven ribbon. Patchwork throws featured heavily, with mirrors sewn in that twinkled under the glimmer of her thousands of fairy lights. Paintings hung on every wall. There were wooden boxes of all sizes and shapes, a mirror with shells plastered over it and spider plants dripping their offspring everywhere. There wasn't a clear inch of wall anywhere.

Spod shook her shoulders, raised her head, cleared her throat and looked pointedly at him as he tried to find a comfortable spot on the cushions.

"We have discovered that your knowledge is terribly lacking in all areas of skimming – or in other words, you know nothing." Spod paced the room while she talked. Because it was so full this meant moving one foot in either direction. The overall result was swaying on the spot.

Adam tried not to giggle.

"We have lots to cover. I have a notebook for you and a variety of study aids."

She handed him a biro decorated with pink feathers and paper stapled together.

Adam wrote his name on the front of the pad and smiled at her encouragingly.

THERE ARE THREE KEY SETS OF PEOPLE.

AND THEY ARE..?

CONNECTORS, SKIMMERS, AND THE BOARD.

"Connectors are licensed to skim people over a certain distance. I'm working for my license," said Spod. "We follow set routes, guiding skimmers so they don't get lost. The Board provide charts showing suitable hosts."

"Hosts?" Adam asked.

"The people that skimmers visit," she explained. "As skimmers get better, they wear their 'hosts' like badly fitting socks."

Adam put down his pen and stared at Spod.

"What?" he said.

"Apparently it feels all itchy," she said. "I don't really know, I'm only a connector..."

"So you can't skim?" asked Adam.

"Nope. I can only connect. But connectors help skimmers learn to control themselves and pull their minds back in. Like I showed you when I helped you control your bubbles. We put people onto the plain."

"But I can get there without a connector," Adam said.

"That shouldn't be possible Adam."

The teacher-like air had disappeared from Spod's voice.

42

Whatever Spod wanted, Adam saw no compelling reason to confess to this mysterious Board. But he was curious. What would it be like to skim with the help of a connector?

He opened his backpack and pulled out a bar of chocolate.

"What about a deal?" asked Adam, offering Spod a chunk. "You have a go at connecting me first and then I'll talk to the Board."

"Are you crazy? There's no way I'm hooking you up again."

"Save me from myself," Adam said solemnly, "I'll go alone if you don't connect me."

"Our connection was kind of cool, wasn't it?" said Spod.

She coughed away her embarrassment. Adam smiled and put his hand on hers.

"I won't tell anyone," he said.

"Boys," Spod muttered nervously.

"If I do this you have to promise never to skim alone. You could be lost forever."

Adam nodded encouragingly as Spod swept the bed clear and pointed to it.

"Put your feet on my pillow, take your shoes off and put your head here," she said.

She perched next to him and placed her hands deep into his hair, palms firmly on his skull. The warmth tickled his ears.

"Close your eyes," Spod directed, "and don't speak unless you're in trouble."

Adam settled himself onto the bed. He concentrated on locating himself – placing Spod's bed in her house, on the road, in the town.

"Stop," Spod pulled back. "What are you doing?"

"I'm locating myself."

"Awesome. How?"

"Well," Adam was embarrassed. "I locate where I am pretty easily, street, town, universe and then I do the same with time. That's a bit harder, I use markers."

"Phenomenal," gasped Spod, spitting the word out. "But this time don't do anything. I'm connecting you remember?"

Adam did as he was told, struggling to remain thoughtless. The back of his neck prickled and a teasing ache spread underneath his skull. The pressure intensified, but this was different. She cocooned her thoughts around his. Her breath was slow and deep, his slowed down to match. She caught his consciousness, crushed it into a ball and threw it with all her might into the first host. Adam shot forward.

Adam knew every thought in the driver's head – including his opinion of people who drove the wrong way down streets.

It was a continuous stream of thoughts.

"That blasted indicator! Who's been fiddling with the seat? What's this? Road's closed for drainage works!"

Adam had just adjusted to being in motion and the sensation of his hands on the wheel when he was shot forward again.

"Pull up the hose," shouted a hoarse voice.

The person he was now in was looking down into a drain, there was toilet paper in large clumps and a deadly odour. This person wasn't saying much, he was focused on the drain.

Adam gagged and then flexed slightly. He pushed to feel more but he was slammed back into his own body.

"What are you doing?" Spod leaned over him, their noses almost touching. Adam smiled.

"Nothing," he lied. "I'm about to puke." He sat up and retched repeatedly into a waste paper bin she handed him, and sipped from a glass of water. It was obvious she'd seen it all before.

"When I'm connecting you, I lead," Spod said. "Which means that you, as a tourist, look, listen and learn. You do not join in. Let me make this very clear. Do not probe other people."

Adam looked up at her and smiled in what he considered was a winning manner.

"You're awesome," he said. "I can go out to a host and then back to my body. But you sent me to two people."

"That's connecting," Spod said theatrically. "And that's your lot for today. It's too dangerous without the Board's permission."

"But it's, it's, it's..." words failed Adam. What he really wanted to say was 'fun', but that seemed a bit lame.

"I promise to be good if we go again," he said contritely.

"And you promise never to skim alone?" Spod asked.

"That too," Adam replied, taking her hand and kissing it gallantly.

"Hmm," she said, as a broad grin lit up her face.

Chapter eight

ADAM HADN'T MEANT TO BREAK HIS PROMISE NOT TO SKIM ALONE. He'd kept it for a couple of days, but he couldn't help himself. After all, skimming wasn't a crime like stealing, or murder. Nevertheless, he was careful to conceal the truth from Spod.

He really liked it when she connected him and he definitely didn't want that silvery light to stop, even if the hosts she chose to visit were as dull as ditch water. She could move him between people and that was pretty cool. By himself, it was as if he was a kid who couldn't aim properly and splashed deep into the water on the first throw, whereas she could send him skimming across host after host. As much as he loved what she could do, it really annoyed him that he couldn't do it alone.

Adam lay on his bed and attempted to ignore the ghastly sound of Marion singing outside his bedroom door.

He wanted to skim further than he'd been before. He didn't need distractions, he needed quiet to make a giant leap. Spod could connect him between several minds – proper skimming – now he was trying to increase his distance.

He'd already visited everyone on his street – it was time to turn the corner and see how far he could get. He'd decided on just the person to visit: Mr Williams.

Adam vaguely knew Mr Williams. He was one of the people his parents made him say 'hello' to every time they saw him, by poking Adam in his back.

"It's important to show sympathy," Adam's mother always told him, "he's been through so much." Adam remembered it well.

Mr Williams' wife and three children had been killed in a car accident about a year or so ago. Hannah, Imogen and Henry had shared a funeral. Adam's teacher had shared the newspaper clipping around the class.

ampion

Vol 19

deals Comic Jim drops in on

THREE CHILDREN KILLED IN TRAGIC ACCIDENT

Report by
Laura Martin

YESTERDAY a mother and kids were squashed out of existence when a lorry overturned on their car. "It was freaky", said a by-stander. "The lorry tipped right over when it was turning on the round-about. There was nothing anyone could do, they died instantly."

What the newspaper had failed to report, according to school rumours, was that at the exact second of his family's death, Mr Williams had cried out in anguish, clutching his head. Since then he was often heard mumbling to himself in a distinctive rasp.

If Adam could make it to Mr Williams, it would be the furthest he'd been. He relaxed and let the familiar sensations run through his body as he entered the dark plain. He missed the loose energy of the golden bubbles, but now that Spod had taught him to harness their power he wasn't going to let them spill out again. He shot forward into the darkness, and felt a small surge of pride at covering such a distance and keeping his body together so neatly.

This host was definitely a man, Adam could tell by the smell of sour sweat that draped across the heavy air. A light humming came from all around, like bees caught in lavender. He felt as if he was breathing musty velvet. Was he in the right person?

Adam pushed his mind out, testing the ground that he was metaphorically standing upon. There was something missing, like the host wasn't at home, a lack of awareness. Adam was instinctively cautious about this person. Was his new host asleep? or... He couldn't think of what else might cause this lack of activity, except death. But this guy was buzzing.

He reached his arms out into the blackness, trying to get some idea of whether this was Mr Williams or not. The velvety air caressed his skin, it was lightly supporting him which was a little freaky. He pushed forward into the dark, testing the strength of the warm mush.

Mr Williams' rasping voice was unmistakable. Adam was where he'd wanted to be – but now he didn't want to be there at all. The darkness tightened around him, he couldn't move. The air gripped every part of him and he knew without a doubt that his body, back home on his bed, had started sweating.

"I'm not going to let you go until you speak to me," Mr Williams said. "Identify yourself!"

Adam didn't dare breathe. Nobody had noticed him before. He didn't know what to do. His body spasmed in his room before his lungs stopped pumping.

"Your body will die shortly," Mr William's said. "If you want to live, tell me who you are."

"Adam Barnes," the words wheezed out. The darkness pulled back, his body gasped for air on his Spiderman duvet.

Adam jumped, propelled by an overwhelming fear.

Eyes screwed shut, Adam didn't look where he was going. When he stopped moving he opened his eyes in panic. This wasn't his body, instead he was in a woman, pegging out her washing on a line, struggling against the fierce wind.

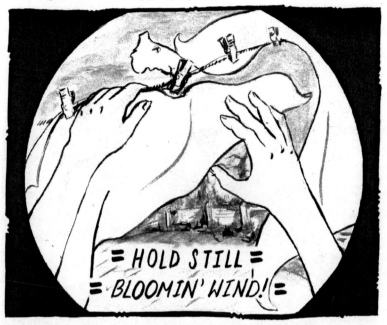

The woman raised her fist in frustration shaking it at the sky, Adam saw what he needed. A recognisable landmark. The back of his house, just a few doors down the road. He placed himself and then he was gone – fleeing back into his own mind.

When his body was done retching, Adam gulped a pint of water. His head pounding, shivering with cold and totally exhausted, he curled up under the duvet.

A smile ran across his lips. As scary as it had been, he had skimmed – properly – by himself. His pure panic, forgetting he had a body, had unleashed what he had craved for so long. The ability to skim between different minds without the assistance of Spod. So what if he'd been seen by Mr Williams? He hadn't been caught.

Chapter nine

ALTHOUGH ADAM WAS BURSTING TO DISCUSS HIS EXPERIENCES, SPOD COULD NEVER KNOW WHAT HAD HAPPENED. Telling her about Mr Williams and his skimming trip would mean admitting he'd lied and gone alone. So when he stepped into her bedroom, instead of laying on her bed to get connected, he sat on the floor amongst the piles of soft toys. He was worried that Mr Williams might be out there, waiting.

Spod lifted herself from the fan of papers on the bed and pushed her wayward hair behind her ears to cover her disappointment.

"I'm tired," Adam offered with a wan smile. It was all the encouragement she needed.

"That's no excuse," she said. "Let's go."

Adam sighed. She was as addicted as him. Sometimes it was easier to give in to Spod than to fight her, and anyway he'd escaped from Mr Williams the last time.

She placed her hands in his hair and began. The first host was bland – the same as all the Board's hosts. Adam didn't bother to look around, he knew she'd move him quickly, once, twice, three times, skimming at speed through a series of monotonous minds. Every so often Adam began to pay attention as Spod landed him in an interesting host rather than the regular dulls that the Board served up. Spod was stretching her powers.

Adam was about to ask her to slow down so that he could get a proper look, when he noticed he was being followed. At first it was just a sensation. Then it was fact. Looking back he could see a dark form running to catch him, using Spod's connection to chase him down.

Adam crouched down and willed Spod to hurl him forward, faster and faster, skimming him from mind-to-mind. He cried out as dread overwhelmed him:

The figure behind ran at full tilt, leaping between hosts, intent on catching his prey.

Adam screamed. With a gut wrenching thud, he was back in his body.

"Are you alright?" Spod asked, concern in her eyes.

Adam threw up, and then wiped away the mucus dribbling out of his nose.

"I was being chased."

"By the Board?"

"How would I know?" Adam answered.

"I bet it was," she said. "Now we're in trouble. Come on."

She put her hands on his shaking head once more.

"Are you mad?" Adam asked. "I'm not going back."

"Yes you are," Spod said. "Or they'll come here."

Adam had no choice. He left his body dangling over the bucket and joined her on the dark plain. Their silvery connection glowed in the darkness.

"It's the Board," Spod whispered, "Let me do the talking."

Adam looked at where she was pointing. The man that had chased him had been joined by an elderly lady. The woman was fishing for something in her pocket. She pulled out a handful of silvery keys.

The woman turned one of the keys purposefully in front of Adam. A lock flickered briefly around it before disappearing.

"Shush," said the woman in response to Spod's spluttering indignation. She raised another key and Spod was silenced.

The woman turned to the man beside her.

"Tell Mr Williams that his request has been granted," she said.

Adam looked at his shoes, he had been caught and he'd paid the price. No, his little sister Marion had paid the price.

Adam sighed as he remembered the last time he'd seen Spod. She'd been standing next to Marion's body. Tears in her eyes.

He brushed the image away, determined not to let the memories distract him.

"How did lockdown feel exactly?" the Questioner asked.

"It's like a fishing net over your head, pulled tightly inwards," Adam said eventually. "It squeezes your thoughts together, and freezes your personality."

The Questioner smiled and nodded as if this was a natural occurrence.

"Lockdown takes your consciousness from the size of the universe, to the size of a pea. Your brain can't move. If you think, you'll snap."

Silence filled the air between them.

"Is that exact enough?" asked Adam curtly.

Chapter ten

ADAM AWOKE, HIS HEAD POUNDING. He rolled over and sat up.

She didn't respond. He put his hand gently over her mouth, her breathing was shallow.

Adam stroked Spod's hand lightly. He didn't know what to do now. Was this what lockdown was like? He knew the facts, but they were cloudy. He couldn't force his mind to think creatively about what to do next. He couldn't come up with a single idea. There was no energy for problem solving, no emotion about what had happened, nothing. A whisper of him said something about being a host now, but then that was gone too.

Adam made his way home slowly.

The Board might have locked his mind down but they couldn't control his limbs – seemingly.

His house was a hive of activity. Police and people milled around in a sea of urgency. He pushed his way through and climbed the stairs to his bedroom.

A policeman stopped Adam, eyeing him suspiciously.

"When did you last see your sister?" the officer asked.

"I don't know," Adam replied. Later the police asked more questions – about Marion's friends and what she liked doing. He couldn't answer those either. His mum grabbed him.

"Think Adam!" she cried, "This is urgent. Marion's vanished!"

The Questioner sighed whilst Adam collected his thoughts.

"So I shook mum off and went to bed. The next morning, I went to school. Then I came home and failed to answer more questions about Marion. It felt like I was underwater. I was hearing things but I couldn't make sense of any of the individual sounds."

"Go on," said the Questioner. "Tell me what happened with Williams."

"I bumped into him three weeks later. It was raining, really heavily, and he just stood there looking at me with a weird grin on his face," said Adam.

Rain dripped from Adam's hair and into his face, blurring his vision. He wiped the water from his eyes.

"I heard about your sister going missing," said Williams. "Do the police have any idea who's taken her?"

Adam's stomach churned with remembered fear as the sound of Williams' cold laughter hit him like a slap in the face. When Williams walked away, still laughing, there was nothing Adam could do but follow. At least fear was an emotion – it was a long time since he'd felt anything. It stirred his curiosity.

Adam sped up and stomped along behind the older man until they entered a familiar road. Williams walked up to his front door, opened it and disappeared inside.

Adam did the only thing that his limited brain could manage – he knocked on the door. Williams opened it with a frown. He'd already taken off his jacket and the shirt underneath was lightly crumpled. There were faint sweat marks under his armpits and his tie flapped awkwardly.

Adam pushed past the older man into the hallway. It was full of memories. Photos of children lined the wall.

Mr Williams took Adam by the arm, halting him. Then he held a finger up and moved it slowly from side to side, whilst observing Adam's eyes following the movement.

"Go in," he said, opening a door off the hallway into a small room lined with a books and framed maps.

Adam's belly oozed with anxiety. It was better than feeling nothing.

"Your lockdown's breaking. I need to make a call."

Williams left the room, locking the door from the outside.

Adam stood up, rattled the handle and pulled hard. The door didn't budge. He should sit down and close his eyes – take a rest. That would be a good decision.

Adam's heart lurched, he'd made a decision. When was the last time that had happened?

Immediately an intense thumping pain started above his eyes, and nausea hit, swelling up from the bottom of his belly as if to throw up his fear. He grabbed a metal wastepaper bin and retched.

The door opened. Mr Williams, giving a running commentary into his mobile, looked down in disgust.

"Listen, to me. He's in my house. You need to deal with it," said Williams. "Do it properly this time. I don't want him crawling round my head."

With that he snapped his phone shut and left. The lock clicked ominously.

Adam managed to pull himself into a chair. He shut his eyes. Now he was upright, his head thumped less. It would be best to go to sleep for a minute, to relax and stop fighting. He was obviously ill, he needed to recover.

He leaned back and concentrated on the deliciousness of giving up. There were no more feelings of fear, there was no more decision making. There was time to simply be, in this room, in this house, in this road, right now.

In that moment, the one nano-second that Adam located who, where and why he was, his absolute uselessness in time and space, his brain exploded into ferocious life. Despair, hate, love, anticipation, pity, joy, greed, lust, envy, compassion, curiosity, coursed through him. Adam's lockdown had failed. Now he had to get out of this house.

Adam wrenched the front door open but Williams was on him, grabbing his arms and kicking the door shut. He struggled, trying to rip his way out of Williams' grasp, not knowing whether to protect his body or his mind.

Adam kicked, bit, scratched and punched, but Williams held on, smiling grimly.

In desperation Adam relaxed into Williams's arms, letting his body go limp. Mr Williams, taken by surprise, loosened his grip. Adam fell to his knees, between his opponent's arms, and scuttled backwards across the hall before running up the stairs.

He darted into a bedroom. The street below was empty and the rain-spattered window was fastened.

Williams was coming up the stairs, clunking his way, not in a hurry, calling his name. Adam looked around for a weapon. He had no way to defend himself or jam the door shut.

Adam looked out of the window. A woman was getting out of a car. This was it, his only hope. He pounded on the glass but she didn't look round. She was too busy unloading her groceries, her head deeply immersed in the boot.

He sprinted across the room to almost within Williams' grasp, and then turning on the spot, he charged at the window. He had no choice.

Adam's mind was already gone, skimming into the woman with her bags of shopping.

"Look round!" he commanded, "Help the boy!"

He skimmed onwards, past an old man (who watched Mr Williams rush out of the house and lean over Adam's broken body). Adam skimmed faster, up the road and into the relative safety of his mother's head. He left no trail, he had no connector, no one was able to follow him.

Chapter eleven

"I WROTE MOST OF THEM RETROSPECTIVELY," ADAM SAID. "The sixth rule is 'protect yourself mentally'."

"And that means?" the Questioner asked.

"Live with the truth in the best way that you can. That's what I had to do next, to cope with getting to know my mum."

Adam paced around the empty stadium. Who would have guessed that his mother's mind was this desolate? The arena no longer had grass, just baked mud. Once, bands ruled this stage but now it was abandoned. Litter rustled in the breeze.

The swing seats were rusted into the upright position. The only sign of life was a flickering screen: the backdrop to whatever act was on stage. It showed whatever his mother saw, and right now she was looking at Adam's bandaged body in hospital.

His Mum covered her eyes, blacking out Adam's view. She sighed, the noise reverberated around the arena until it sounded as if the stands would collapse in despair. She already had one missing child, she couldn't cope with losing another.

The wind nipped at Adam, pushing him back to the sidelines as a single word – 'Marion' – boomed repeatedly through the stadium's speakers. Why wasn't his mum calling his name?

Adam retreated to the back of the stadium, next to a run-down burger stall. Even with his hands clamped to his ears Adam couldn't block out her despair. Or his own. She didn't care about him. She wanted him out of the way so that she could concentrate her worry on one child.

He shivered. There was only one cure for his mother's desolation. He had to find Marion, dead or alive.

But how? There was no point going back into his physical body. It was weak and cut up from the fall. His skimming body, which could go from a golden blur to a beefier version of himself with better hair, was fine. But it was not the same as having muscular power and he desperately missed the familiar solidity of a physical body.

He had to move into a host who would help him. Someone who would understand the hitchhiker in their brain and keep him safe from the Board – someone named Spod. Adam vowed to take the first opportunity to get to her.

When the doorbell roused his mother from wiping the same plate for the 37th time, he knew this was the moment. Whoever was on the other side of the door was about to get skimmed.

The man's mind was fresh, full of electric energy. He introduced himself to Adam's mother as a police detective but Adam didn't catch his name. He was too busy adjusting to the furious pace of the detective's mind.

This room was tiny compared to his mother's stadium. At its centre, a vortex of light swirled with glittering colours. The vortex sent out tendrils to tap the fronts of filing cabinets where the detective stored his cases. One wall was dominated by a screen with hundreds of programs that filtered the detective's thought processes. It also had a live feed.

Adam leant against a cabinet, while ducking away from tendrils that whipped around him.

He watched as his mum asked about the topic that was always on her mind.

The detective was asking if Adam had regained consciousness yet. A few loose ends needed to be tied up about Adam's fall from the bedroom window of Mr William's house.

Discarded flyers began to float around his mum's stadium, little bits of litter, labelling him: a thief, a housebreaker.

It was plausible. His pockets had been stuffed with Williams' possessions when his body was admitted to hospital. What could he say to defend himself without being carted off in a straight-jacket? Lockdowns, Boards and skimming weren't common words in police vocabulary.

Adam's mum answered the detective's questions in a monotone manner, not inviting him into her house, she had no interest in defending Adam and remained mute when the detective asked about his friends. And then to Adam's horror, she started to close the door in the detective's face.

Adam had to move fast.

If the detective visited Spod's house, Adam could skim straight into Spod's mind, saving precious time.

He placed himself and skimmed, for the last time he hoped, back into his mother.

"What was the policeman's name?" asked the Questioner.

"I never found out," Adam hung his head miserably. "I couldn't exactly ask him."

"That must be one of your rules, no interference?"

"Number seven," said Adam. "Don't mess with your host."

"I bet you did though, didn't you?" the Questioner said slyly. "That's why you look so nervous. You know right from wrong don't you? Maybe not, after all, we both know what you did to Marion. Yes, I know your little secret. We'll get to that later."

Adam rose shakily. "I don't have to listen to this," he said.

"You have nowhere else to go. Sit down. Tell me about the detective. What happened next?"

"I was in the detective's mind, trying to avoid the tendrils. I could hear him getting annoyed with mum."

"Mrs Barnes? Are you okay?" the detective sighed.

"Never mind about me," snapped Adam's mother. "Just you let me know if you hear anything about Marion."

His mum shut the door firmly and left the detective staring at the peeling paint.

A lone tendril swung by Adam's head and touched the cabinet with his name on, closing off interest. His plan of getting to Spod was going awry. He had to make a move.

Adam squatted on the floor to avoid the flailing tendrils. He blew on his hands where they'd been burnt.

The detective slumped against Adam's front door, hitting the door bell. His mum swung the door open glaring angrily at the detective.

"Leave me alone," she said tersely.

Chapter twelve

As soon as the detective knocked, Spod's mother opened her door. Dark rings circled her red eyes. The end of her nose was raw from blowing her misery away.

Peering through the tendrils flexing around in the detective's mind, Adam tried to focus on the images. It was difficult. They faded in and out but at last he could make out the familiar figure of the detective in conversation with Spod's mother.

As he watched the detective gently ease Spod's bedroom door open, Adam gasped in horror. Lockdown had hit her hard, both mentally and physically. She lay on her bed, her eyes glazed. Dribble oozed from the corner of her mouth. The thought of taking up temporary residence in her quickly lost its appeal.

"She's been like this for weeks," Spod's mum sobbed from the doorway.

The detective put his hand out to the girl. As his fingers touched her cheek, a razor of electricity seared into his mind and jolted through Adam.

Adam jumped to his feet and grabbed a tendril to steady himself. Electricity shot through him again. The detective crumpled onto Spod's floor unable to cope with the spiking agony in his head.

Adam skimmed into Spod: as bad as she looked on the outside, she was a better bet as a host than the detective.

Now he stood on the edge of a wide, grey circular room. Waterfalls thundered from ceiling to floor in front of him, enclosing a burning ball of fire. Dazzling colours: reds; purples; and oranges danced in the drenching spray.

There was no doubt in Adam's mind that the fire was Spod — an angry, locked down Spod. He peered through the water at her burning centre. Like this, she was truly beautiful but there wasn't time to think about that now, the heat was already causing his skin to tighten and blister.

"You're locked down," Adam yelled, "But you can get out."

Spod's flames moved warily inside the cage. She backed into the water, steam encasing her. She stretched herself, filling the cage. Then she started spinning, gradually building up speed. Spurts of steam erupted whenever she touched the water.

Adam scrambled back. He'd thought it'd been hot before, but this was intense, he was being roasted.

Crouching down to shield himself from the heat, Adam's flesh began to crack. The raw stench of his body cooking filled his nose. He went to wipe the sweat from his forehead, but there was no more moisture left to come out of his skin.

"Don't worry about me," he croaked, "it's not real. It's all in our heads. Keep going."

Spod did as she was told, turning faster and faster, curling flames out into the water, forcing it to change. She was angry, burning, unstoppable.

Steam rose hissing in protest, billowing with the effort of trying to remain liquid.

Wetness enveloped Adam, filling his mouth as he tried to find air. He was drowning, Spod's fire had consumed all the oxygen. He tried to call her name, but his gurgling throat closed.

On the bed, Spod's body arched, she opened her mouth. Waves and waves of black steam exploded from her.

`"You're okay," Spod's mum kept saying, repeating the words to make herself believe them.

As the detective pulled into the hospital car park, Spod winced. She needed to get Adam's unconscious skimming body out of her head before it had dire consequences for them both.

"I'll see a doctor later mum," she said as she pushed through the hospital entrance. "Honestly I'm okay."

In the Critical Care Unit, Adam's real body lay motionless. The surgeon had picked the shattered glass from William's window out of his face. But all attempts to reach him had failed.

Spod stopped abruptly at Adam's ward and a nurse ushered her in. The white sheet draped over Adam made him look like he was already dead, even though the machines were keeping him alive. Pulling a chair in from the corridor, Spod sat as close to Adam's bed as she could and gently held his hand.

Spod gulped down the lump in her throat as the door clicked shut. She brushed the hair off Adam's forehead, and kissed him.

"This is it," she whispered, and crossed her fingers. There was only one thing she could think of doing to shock him back.

Spod flicked the switches to 'off' and placed her hands on Adam's head. She put her forehead to his and slipped inside his mind.

Threads of Adam's personality hung from the ceiling, wafting around her as she moved. They were all muddy brown. He was shutting down, there was even less time than she'd hoped.

"Adam?" she whispered. "Get back here."

His heart stopped beating, the light faded.

Spod shivered then gently touched one of the threads. It carried a dull memory of Adam's smell. She touched a couple more, running pieces of him through her hands. His laughter. His smile.

"Adam?" she called, louder. "Stop messing with me."

His blood stopped flowing.

Spod yelled, grabbing at the threads, trying to find one with life attached, before she got dragged into his body's death.

ADAM! WHERE ARE YOU?

Then Spod felt it, one thread pulsed in response to her touch.

Brushing the others aside she grabbed it and pulled gently. It grew brighter in the warmth from her hands. She heaved on it, trying to pull his skimming self back into his own mind, ignoring the faint shouts from outside.

As the nurse pulled Spod off Adam, she was hoiked back into her own mind. She slumped defeated onto the chair, her connection broken. Nurses scrambled around, one flicking switches on the machines, another pumping on Adam's chest.

"I told you it was all in your head," were the only words Adam said before falling into a deep sleep.

Adam awoke an hour later. His head was thumping, but it felt good to be back in his own body. His limbs felt stiff after many days of non-use. Spod, after grudgingly seeing a doctor, had left the hospital. The detective, however, had not.

As soon as Adam's eyes opened, the detective started asking questions. Was Adam going to admit to burgling Mr Williams' house? What did he know about Marion's disappearance?

Adam listened intently as the detective talked. The first missing girl was Michelle Tennant, 14. She disappeared a couple of weeks before Marion. She had thin, blonde hair, and green eyes.

Before he was locked down, Adam had heard she'd run away. Now, with the other girls gone, the police were getting suspicious. The second child was Marion. Lovely, brainy, irritating Marion.

The third was Evie Goldsmith, aged eight. Youngest, smallest, snottiest. Her eyes watered constantly with hay fever.

All three girls had gone missing. Michelle had never returned from a trip to the corner shop. Evie was taken from behind her mother's back at the park. Marion had told her parents she was going out to play, but she never came home.

The Questioner smirked. "You sent Marion straight there. Why didn't you tell the detective that?"

Adam scratched his eyebrow. The simple truth was he didn't remember. He'd been trapped in Spod's mind, half-burnt and then pulled back from death. Then he'd woken up in the hospital to the sound of the detective going on and on about the burglary. How was he expected to remember a conversation he'd had with Marion weeks before?

Chapter thirteen

"I'M STILL WONDERING WHETHER TO ARREST YOU," THE DETECTIVE SAID CASUALLY, "BUT MR WILLIAMS DOESN'T WANT TO PRESS CHARGES."

"I'm not a burglar," said Adam.

"The ambulance men found valuables in your pocket belonging to Mr Williams' dead wife. All the man wants is an apology."

The detective flicked a grape into his mouth.

"I'm not speaking to him," said Adam. "I didn't do anything. You can't make me."

The detective sighed. "It's a bit late for that..."

"I'll get a coffee," the detective said, rising to his feet.

Williams sat down in the chair and folded his hands in his lap.

"Feeling better?" he laughed as the door closed.

"I didn't steal anything," said Adam, trying to keep the tremor out of his voice.

"I know," Mr Williams said. "I stuffed your pockets with my dead wife's jewellery and told the police that you were a burglar."

He paused, and licked the inside of his mouth, as if anticipating the flavour of his next words.

"Never come to my home or speak to me again. If you do I'll have you locked down for good."

Adam cringed. Williams wasn't finished.

"I will put your head in a vice and turn it until blood pours out of your ears," said Williams. "Like this."

A hot pyramid of glass carved a path through Adam's head.

"No more skimming," the older man muttered, exploding

the pyramid and sending shards of glass splintering through Adam's consciousness.

Mr Williams loosened his grip on Adam.

"Good," he said and began removing the glass from Adam's mind, piece by piece, as the door opened.

The detective swore on the way through the door, he'd just dripped coffee down his shirt.

Williams took a step back and excused himself as he left the room, shutting the door behind him.

"You apologised?" The detective asked.

Adam ignored him. One tiny piece of glass remained in his mind, an itching reminder from Mr Williams. It wasn't real, he could control this pain if he concentrated.

Adam probed the glass, attempting to push it out. But as he touched it, his gut churned. Williams' power was intertwined with a trace of someone else – Marion.

If Marion was still alive, she needed him now. And if she was dead? It was time to find out.

"Stop lying," the Questioner said.

Adam sat in surly silence. It had been an accident!

When Michelle Tennant had disappeared, Adam had told his sister that Mr Williams had kidnapped her. Back then it had been a ridiculous joke. Williams was just a sad, lonely man. Adam didn't expect Marion to actually go to Williams' house to look for the missing girl. But that's exactly what his headstrong sister had gone and done. It was not his fault.

"What happened next?" the Questioner demanded.

"The detective gave me a ride home from hospital," said Adam. 'When I got back, Spod was waiting for me."

Chapter fourteen

Spod sat on Adam's old duvet cover. He'd thought it looked childish before but now he didn't care.

"I know where Marion went," Adam said urgently.

"Where?" asked Spod.

It was time for the truth. All of it. He'd gone skimming alone when he'd promised her he wouldn't. He'd told Marion that Williams was the kidnapper and she'd gone to his house to spy on him. Then Williams appeared at the hospital to warn him off.

Spod listened, alternating between reassurance and spitting anger at Adam's stupidity.

"I need you to connect me," Adam said finally.

She slumped back against the wall, eyeing him angrily.

"No way," she snapped. "Why risk reminding the Board we're here? I want to find Marion, but I can't live through another lockdown. Skim by yourself!"

"It's too dangerous," Adam replied, "I need your help."

"Skimming is the only way to find her," Adam pleaded.

"No!" Spod said. "We'll go to his house. Look for evidence of Marion. Then the police will have to believe you."

Pulling on her jacket, she grabbed Adam's hand. He shied away and pushed past her towards the door.

"From coma to commando," she sighed.

Adam stopped in the kitchen to say goodbye to his mum. Immersed in a cookbook, she didn't look up.

Five minutes later, Adam and Spod sauntered past Mr Williams' house, trying to appear casual. His car wasn't outside and the property seemed empty.

"I'll keep watch," Spod said. "You go and look."

A thin path ran down the side of the house leading to an iron gate which gave access to the back garden. Adam ducked around the wheelie bins and reached the gate. It was rusted shut; choking flowers poked through from pots on the other side.

Adam glanced around. A conservatory, covered in vines, ran along the back of the house. He moved closer, pushing aside a withered bunch of grapes to peer in through the dirty glass.

Tatty magazines and piles of clothes were strewn on the floor and wind chimes hung silent across the internal door. A group of chairs with lumpy cushions on them was arranged around a table with a stack of fly-infested plates on it. He thrust the grape vines aside to coax more light in through the window.

Then Adam realised that the 'cushions' weren't actually cushions – they were people. Filthy dirty children, food crusted on their faces, their hair matted, slumped barefoot in the armchairs.

Adam's stomach churned at the sight of the missing girls.

Their heads were held at uncomfortable angles. And Marion was in the centre, her eyes shut, her mouth open. A fly landed on her face but she didn't react when it crawled across her lips.

Adam banged furiously on the glass but his sister didn't move a muscle.

"Marion," he shouted, banging again.

It was useless. He ran back to the gate and grabbed a plant pot, ready to smash his way in.

At the end of the path, Spod was signalling frantically. Adam ignored her and strode back to the conservatory. He would break in, get Marion and then what? Take her body home? Call an ambulance?

Adam ducked down, dropping the plant pot on the ground beside him and peered in through the vines.

Williams cleared the dishes, then attended to the girls. He did this tenderly, washing their faces and hands before patting them dry with a tea towel. None of them responded.

After admiring his work, Williams linked the girls hands in a semi-circle. He tied their wrists to each other with green ribbon. That done, he placed one of his hands on top of Marion's and gave the other to a girl that Adam guessed was Evie, completing the circle.

Mr Williams tugged at the girls' hands, pulling them to their feet. He smiled gently around the group, casting hungry, loving glances at their blank faces.

The girls' movements were spasmodic, erratic, as if Mr Williams was their puppet master. He forced Marion's arm upwards into the air. The motion ran around the circle. It was like watching macabre street-dancers doing the hokey-cokey.

Adam bit his cheek, hoping to check his nausea. Hot blood filled his mouth, its iron scent burning in his nose. He kept his eyes firmly on Marion. She juddered unsteadily, as if standing was new to her and she needed to practice. Her eyes were screwed shut the whole time.

Adam found himself staring into the eyes of his sister's body. But it wasn't Marion looking back.

Chapter fifteen

SPOD HELPED ADAM OVER WILLIAMS' GARDEN GATE. His arm caught on one of its rusty iron tips. She looked in horror at the blood seeping through Adam's shirt, and pursed her lips.

"We're going to my house," she whispered firmly.

Safely in her bedroom, Spod pressed a tissue against the cut.

"Call the police," she said. "They'll have to believe you now."

Adam grabbed Spod by the shoulders, forcing her head up.

"I told you" he hissed. "There's someone else living in Marion's body. They'd arrest Williams and rescue the girls but then what? It's not my sister in that body! You have to connect me so I can find the real Marion."

Spod shook his hands off, and threw away the bloody tissue.

"The Board will be waiting to lock us down as soon as you start skimming," she said. "Which means no one will ever find out that Williams has got three kidnapped girls."

"That's exactly what my sister's like now!" Adam snapped kicking a pile of soft toys that lay on the floor. Spod snatched up a yellow rabbit and caressed it.

"Sorry," Adam said guiltily, slumping on her bed. "I'm wound up."

"And I'm not?" Spod's eyes flashed. "We'll only have seconds before the Board turn up."

"We'll make them listen," said Adam confidently.

"You'd better," Spod said. She pushed Adam down and dug her fingernails into his temples.

"That hurts," Adam grunted.

Spod let go. She got up, crossed the room and pressed her nose to the glass gazing at the street.

"I can't do it. I can't face another lockdown."

Adam followed her to the window. He put his arms around her and pulled her back to him.

"It's okay," he whispered. "The Board will listen. They have to." He patted her hair clumsily. It smelled of lime.

"I'm frightened," Spod said. She turned to face him and laid her head on his shoulder.

"So am I," Adam said, hugging her tightly. "But I owe it to Marion to find her. You're the only one who can help me."

They clung together for minutes until Spod moved. She placed both her hands deeply in Adam's hair and tilted her head up.

"Okay?" she asked, stretching up to press her lips against his.

Adam couldn't resist, he kissed her back. This wasn't meant to happen, not when Marion needed him, not when his mouth tasted of blood. His first kiss was with Spod. Spod of all people.

She jerked back abruptly.

"Are you ready?" Spod asked as the familiar skimming sensations swirled through Adam's mind. And then they stood on Adam's dark plain, leaving their bodies locked together in Spod's room.

The Board were there in seconds. It was almost as if they'd been waiting for the pair to appear. Walking through the darkness came hundreds of them, men and women. Each Board member wore a smart blazer. The men had a sprig of white heather in their lapels and the women wore lilies.

The figures melted into one another until there were just two Board members in front of Adam and Spod, each holding a key. Two shimmering locks appeared.

"Stop!" Adam yelled.
The man shook his head slowly.

"No second chances," he said, raising a key towards Adam.

"If you do this, it'll be the end of the Board," yelled Spod furiously. "The hosts whose brains you've fried with your skimming experiments. All the people who hear voices in their heads. Everyone will know your dirty secrets."

Adam stared at Spod in confusion – she was impressive in her fury.

"I've put together a file, all about the Board and its activities. If anything happens to me – like lockdown – it'll go viral."

Spod stared at Adam as if to say, "Don't contradict me."

"Turn that key and the Board's over," hissed Spod.

The woman laughed loudly.

"The point of blackmail," she said, "is to have leverage. The government know all about us, and what we do. They fund our research."

The woman glanced uneasily at the man.

"Williams has kidnapped my sister," explained Adam. "And two other girls."

"He's starting a collection," added Spod.

"He's got Marion's body but her mind has gone. God knows what he's done with it."

The woman frowned, choosing her words carefully.

"Mr Williams is no longer connected to us."

"I don't care," said Adam. "I want Marion back. If you lock me down again I'll never find her."

"Enough!" said the man, pointing at Spod. "First you try

blackmail and now you're accusing Williams of this. Do you take us for fools?"

"Check out his conservatory," answered Spod.

"Very well," the woman said. "You have three hours to find your sister. If you're not back by then, we'll be coming. Use your time well, it's the last skimming you'll ever do."

Adam opened his mouth to speak, but Spod was already pulling him back to her room.

"What did you mean back there when you said the Board 'fries minds'?" asked Adam.

Spod made Adam lie on the floor, while she sat behind him on a large pillow.

"Relax," Spod said. It was a command, not a suggestion.

Adam closed his eyes and kept his mouth shut. He had three hours to find Marion. Would that be enough?

100

Chapter sixteen

"GO," SPOD WHISPERED ACROSS THE DARK PLAIN. Adam turned several times, looking for a gleam of light, any host would do. He caught a sliver of blue out of the corner of his eye and he was off, gaining speed, skimming through minds. If the real Marion was out there, still alive, he would find her. Spod trailed out behind, their connection a thick silvery stream. He spotted his next host and moved forward to Williams' neighbourhood, finding Marion's body in a few quick skims.

Water dripped in Marion's empty mind. A dark pool with gentle ripples running across its surface took up most of the floor. Adam skirted it and slumped on an overstuffed sofa.

There was no answer. Adam scanned the cave. His sister had gone. He didn't understand. He was inside Marion's body but there was no sign of her real self.

A small hand gripped his leg like a pincer. A young boy had appeared from behind the sofa. His ginger hair shook as shivers racked his thin frame.

"Where's my sister?" Adam demanded curtly.

"I don't know," replied the boy. Then he cocked his head to one side listening carefully. "Daddy's coming!"

"Who are you?" Adam asked. "What's your name?"

"Henry," the boy replied. "Let's play trains. I like trains."

"Henry," Adam said softly, "do you know your last name?"

"It's Williams," said the little boy, "Shall we play trains now?"

But Adam was already gone.

"I had my sister to worry about," Adam retorted.

"I had other people too, when I met you," said the Questioner, pulling off his cap and running his hands through his sweaty hair. "But I still offered you assistance."

"Assistance?" Adam shouted, "You dragged me down here and locked me in with you. I didn't have a choice!"

"There are always choices."

"I choose to go," said Adam, rising to his feet.

The Questioner sighed heavily and put his hands flat on the table. Moisture beaded under his palms in twin pools.

"Sit down," he ordered.

"Why did you come here to the hospital in the first place?" Adam demanded. "How did you know I was here?"

"If you try to leave you'll never know," the Questioner said. "Now, what happened when you left Henry?"

Adam went in circles, keeping close to Marion's body by skimming through Williams' neighbours, until he realised that Spod would pull him back if he didn't do something. He wanted to be there for Marion. He would look until he found her. Unless the Board locked him down or Williams got to him first.

But how was it possible that the little boy, Henry Williams was in Marion's body? Everyone knew what had happened from the newspaper reports.

THREE CHILDREN KILLED IN TRAGIC ACCIDENT

Report by
Laura Martin

YESTERDAY a mother and kids were squashed out of existence when a lorry overturned on their car. "It was freaky", said a by-stander. "The lorry tipped right over when it

Adam skimmed into the next body in the conservatory. It belonged to Evie, the last girl to be kidnapped.

Inside her, everything was droopingly pink, she was quietly wilting like a shrivelled piece of fruit, shrinking into itself.

There was no sign of the real Evie, but a girl with ginger hair like Henry's, tied in two straggly plaits down her back, had her face pressed into a wall. Her hands reached up to the ceiling and she was swaying, moaning loudly.

Adam looked at her, bewildered. This was Imogen, one of Henry's sisters. Dead, and yet here she was – living in Evie's body. A horrible pattern was occurring.

104

He skimmed into the third girl, the body of Michelle Tennant, and found himself in a corridor peppered with doors.

At the far end of the corridor one door was slightly ajar, a dim glow of light puddling on the floor underneath it.

Edging slowly forward, Adam peered cautiously into the cold grey room. Light came from a solitary bulb. Dank, slimy walls surrounded the muddy floor which had mushrooms sprouting from it. In the centre stood another girl, with shocking ginger hair, hands reaching upwards, eyes shut.

She looked thin and, to Adam's eyes, ill.

With all that ginger hair, she was definitely Hannah Williams.

"I'm looking for my sister," Adam said as she turned to face him. "Your brother Henry's in her body."

"Yes," Hannah said as if this were the most natural thing in the world. She gazed at Adam with interest.

"But as dad says you can't look a gift horse, or girl, in the mouth. Whoever sent Marion to us was very generous. So it's you we need to thank, Marion told me."

In two strides Adam was across the room, grabbing Hannah by the throat and pinning her to the wall.

"Tell me where Marion is or else!"

"Or else what?" Hannah laughed in Adam's face. "You can't threaten the dead. All I need to do is call my daddy and then I'll be the one 'or elsing'."

Adam squeezed tighter, her breath was ragged, coming in fits and spurts but she didn't struggle.

"Where is Marion?"

Hannah's eyes bulged. She smiled, daring him to go further.

Adam stepped back and let her fall to the floor where she lay spread-eagled at his feet. Finally she raised her head.

"That's the most alive I've felt in ages," she said. "Thanks."

Then, as if nothing had happened between them, she sat up and said: "It's Adam isn't it?"

"Where's my sister?" Adam spat.

"I'll tell you," she said, "on one condition. I need a favour."

Adam didn't like the way she smiled as she said this.

"What?" he demanded.

Chapter seventeen

ADAM BACKED AWAY FROM HANNAH. His hand touched the sticky wall of Michelle's empty mind.

"Killing my dad is the price for saving your sister," Hannah said calmly, fixing her eyes on Adam and waiting for an answer.

"Marion's alive?" Adam asked quietly.

"Of course she is," Hannah tutted impatiently. "Dad's got her locked away in his head. For the time being."

"I won't kill anyone," Adam said. "I can't."

"It's the only way to save her. Haven't you figured it out?" Hannah looked at Adam searchingly. "Marion will get her own body back, when you kill dad."

"I haven't figured anything out," Adam said. "Except that you're completely insane."

"Insane? Are you surprised?" Hannah huffed. "Being dead is exhausting, but attempting to come back to life is worse. Day after day, trying to make Michelle's body work. My body died under the lorry. You remember the crash right?"

Adam nodded.

"That's the day I found out dad was experimenting for the Board. Controlling people."

"I can do that," said Adam, trying not to sound proud.

"Dad was skimming the lorry driver, trying to get him to change direction. He did that all right! He made the lorry crash onto our car. But he saved us at the last minute. He grabbed our 'consciousnesses', or whatever you call this," she gestured at herself, "and dragged us out."

"He left mum there when the lorry crashed on top of our car. You know what she was saying? Our names."

Hannah hugged herself.

"Dad's idea of an apology was getting us these new bodies. He makes us practice working them every day. It's not going well. We can't control them by ourselves, so when we're done practicing, he takes us back into his head. We're his prisoners. What kind of afterlife is that? It's teenage torture!"

Adam slumped against the wall. Hannah patted his arm.

"If it makes you feel better," she said. "Henry is doing a good job with Marion's body. He tries really hard. Imogen, on the other hand, is hopeless at controlling Evie. Dad says he'll have to find her another girl to live in soon."

She gripped his hand. "When you get rid of him, I'll be free of all this. Say you'll do it."

She smiled endearingly. The walls started buzzing.

Adam stumbled over a tree root. He'd managed to wrench away from Hannah's grip, but whose mind had he ended up in? He glanced around.

A copse of trees was hemmed by leisurely fields of tulips stretching in every direction. A path dissected the fields and curved towards a stream in the far distance.

Adam raised his face to the sky. It felt good to be away from Williams' crazy daughter, and her murderous demands.

Guiltily, he remembered Spod. She would be waiting in her bedroom, holding his head. He put his hands behind him to their connection, like patting a faithful dog. But she wasn't there. His lifeline was gone and he hadn't even noticed! He peered over his shoulder, looking for the familiar light.

There was still no silver connection. He had no idea where he was, or how to get back. This wasn't skimming, this was sinking.

Chapter eighteen

"YOU NEVER UNDERSTAND," SAID ADAM.

The Questioner coughed and spat phlegm into his hand which he wiped on his trouser leg.

"Adam," he said, "you've brought these children into the tale, Hannah, Imogen and Henry. You say their dad caused a crash and killed them. He stole bodies for them. And Williams' dead daughter wanted her father killed..."

The Questioner put his hands up to his face, holding in another coughing fit. It looked as if he was pushing his sagging cheeks back into place.

"Now you're telling me that you got lost?"

"I've already explained that to skim alone I have to be able to pinpoint my location, in place and time," said Adam. "But I thought Spod was connecting me, so I wasn't looking where I was going. I couldn't skim onwards."

"So what did you do?" the Questioner asked.

Adam stepped out of the copse, forward onto the path, and in two steps he was at the stream, the trees now miles behind him. He squatted down and noticed a bed of white, flat pebbles in the water. Looking closer he realised he could see two shadowy figures in the pool. Did they belong to the reality beyond this mind?

Whoever he was in, was looking at two sleeping children.

That's when it hit him. He was in Hannah. Adam was in a dead girl's consciousness. Was that even possible?

He trailed his hands through the water. Is that why Spod hadn't followed? Because she knew where he'd gone? Or, far more worrying, perhaps Williams had gone after Spod?

Adam knew only too well what Williams was capable of. To stop himself or Spod being hurt, he had to get out of Hannah.

He clambered back from the stream's edge, away from the fish that swarmed around his hand, rudely sucking at his fingertips, and sprinted back to the copse.

"Ah, you've finally worked it out," Hannah whispered, her voice coming from the trees and grass around Adam. Her version of nature rippled when she spoke.

"Smart move coming here, but dad's taken me back to his head, out of Michelle's body, so keep the noise down. I don't want him to know that you're going to do the deed. Murder."

The grass wilted at the word.

"Will you be happy here Adam?"

Hannah's voice rose from the ground and the trees disappeared and were replaced with a bright yellow cornfield.

"What are you talking about?" Adam asked, running his hands through the corn's tassles.

"You're bleeding," Hannah called from the sky.

Adam glanced down. She was right. Blood dripped from his fingers where he'd touched the corn.

"It doesn't hurt," he said.

"Not yet," Hannah replied. Then the corn began to grow. He felt it poking through his jacket and scratching his torso.

He bled freely wherever it touched him.

"Does it hurt now?" Hannah asked sweetly. The sky blackened to midnight blue, and a fierce wind sprung up.

Agonising pain ripped through Adam's sliced skin. He fell to his knees. The corn embraced him, whipping across his face.

Adam screamed. The corn disappeared and he was back in the trees. There wasn't a scratch on him.

"See what I can do?" said Hannah, like an excited tour guide. "Would you like to see some more?"

"Why are you doing this?" Adam yelled.

"Simple. Kill my dad, or stay here with me, in my cornfields."

A sliver of mist rose from the ground and then she was there, standing before him. She looked much better than before, plumper and less tired. She wore a short flowery dress and she'd tied her hair up in a swinging ponytail. When she moved, Adam could see straight through her. She pointed a finger at him.

"You know what?" Hannah said. "If you don't kill dad, I'll ask him if I can have your sister's body instead of Michelle's. I'll keep you here forever, and you can watch me become Marion. When I can control her properly, dad's master plan kicks in. Marion'll be found with no memories of what happened to her. We'll go back to your house in Marion's body. After a while the authorities will come. There'll be charges of neglect against your parents. Marion's body – and us obviously – will be moved to live with a foster family. Guess who that'll be?"

"You can't do that!" Adam shouted.

"I can and I will. That's how dad is going to get his children back to live with him. He's going into fostering."

THE TROUBLE IS, MARION WILL HAVE TO DO SOMETHING REALLY BAD IN ORDER TO GET TAKEN INTO CARE.

WHAT? YOU'RE INSANE!

"Got any ideas?" Hannah asked. "I was thinking we'd get her drunk first and then get her into a gang, carry a knife..."

"That's enough," Adam said defeated.

117

"So you'll do it?" Hannah asked, excitedly clapping her hands. The trees sprouted new leaves around them.

"Help me get back to my body," Adam said, "I'll take the police to your dad's house, he'll be arrested…"

"That's not good enough Adam," Hannah said softly, "Prison won't stop him. He'll be off skimming and we'll be left behind in his locked up body. He has to die."

Adam put his head back against a tree and felt the sharp scratch of its bark against his skull. Hannah positioned herself in front of him and stared into his eyes.

"Not everyone lives happily ever after where skimming is concerned," Hannah said.

"Which means?"

"Adam, I'm going to help you reunite your sister and her body. As soon as you take Marion from his mind, dad'll know. You'll only have a second to get her out, before you finish him off. Otherwise dad's skimming self will be coming after you and I'll be stuck in his dying body. You'll be my knight in shining armour."

Hannah grabbed Adam's hands and kissed them gallantly. He pushed her away.

"What about Michelle and Evie?" he sighed.

"You can't save everyone. There isn't enough time. Anyway they're not your family are they?" Hannah flicked her ponytail. "What are you getting so worked up about?"

Adam hammered his fist against the tree in frustration.

"But I'll be killing them too," he said slowly.

"Only their minds," Hannah said. "Their bodies will be fine. They'll go on and on. But you can save all of Marion, reunite her."

"I'll need to be in my body to do it."

Hannah twirled on the spot, her dress billowing.

"Finally he gets it!" she laughed.

"I need to see my sister and make sure she's okay first."

"I'll connect you," Hannah said. "Otherwise you'll never get out of here. You'll be lost in me and my dad."

Adam shook his head. "Spod's my connector."

"She's gone," Hannah adopted a little girl voice. "I cut her off, when you came here. Don't be cross. She didn't even fight, She just ran away. I'd never leave you like that Adam. You can trust me."

"I doubt it," Adam said, and let her put her hot hands on either side of his head.

Chapter nineteen

ADAM LOOKED AROUND THE ROOM CAUTIOUSLY. Even though Hannah was now his connector, he didn't trust her at all. But she'd done as she said, brought him into Williams' mind, to the stronghold where he locked up his children's consciousness's.

Henry and Imogen lay curled up together, asleep on a floor under a wall covered with pictures of their mother. Hannah fussed around, pulling a blanket over them.

"Look at this," she said. She pointed to the connection swirling between her and Adam. It was black but glittering with a million stars.

"Where's Marion?" Adam asked.

"Take a moment to appreciate our complex skimming situation."

She looked at Adam's furrowed brow.

"Marion?" he demanded.

"Down the hall," Hannah said. "She's got a room to herself. Dad separated her from Michelle and Evie. She caused too much trouble. She's quite something when she starts."

Adam nodded. He edged his way cautiously into the corridor. Hannah shut the door behind him shutting off the comforting circle of light. He ran his hand along the wall. Velvet paper bristled beneath his touch until his fingertips connected with Marion's door handle.

There was no answer. Adam braced himself. He'd changed his shape before, from golden bubbles to a beefier version of himself, but this called for concentration. He stretched himself out into a long series of bubbles intermingling with Hannah's connection and slipped through the key hole.

Marion lay in the corner of the room. Her head was tucked to her knees, and her filthy matted hair hid her face.

"Marion, are you okay?" Adam whispered, putting his hand gently on her shoulder to wake her. "I'm sorry this happened, it's all my fault."

"Yes it is," Marion mumbled without looking up. "I came to tell Mr Williams what you were saying about him being a child snatcher, and he snatched me! Get out of my dream now. It was great, there was a unicorn and ..."

"Marion," Adam interrupted. "You're not dreaming!"

She raised her head slightly.

"You're in Williams' house," he said "sort of."

"I'm not," she said indignantly. "I'm in his brain. That's how I know you're not real. There's no way my pig thick brother would work out how to get here."

IS THAT REAL ENOUGH?

OW!

"Believe me now?" Adam asked and opened his arms. Marion crumpled into him and wept on his chest. When she was done, she stood up.

"Let's go," she said.

Adam pulled her back down. She seemed so small next to him now, as if losing her body had halved her personality.

"Why are we sitting here?" she asked.

"I need to tell you something." Adam pulled her closer, but Marion was distracted, slithering around to look at the streaks of Hannah's light connection from his back.

"I think I can handle complicated skimming stuff. I'm a prisoner in a madman's head. My body's in his conservatory and I've just watched you come through a key hole," Marion said sarcastically.

"Okay then, I'm inside, outside and connected to Hannah," said Adam. "If her dad comes back she'll hide me in her head. But, right now I'm stuck inside Williams too."

"So you're not rescuing me?" Marion asked. "That's not skimming stuff, that's plain mean."

"I'll get you out soon. Really, really soon," Adam said.

"This is a social visit?" Marion's lips pursed. She reminded Adam very much of their mother. Sometimes it was easier to get it over with and tell the truth.

"Listen," said Adam. "I need to get back to my body..."

Adam ducked to avoid her fists as Marion rained small punches onto his head. "You can't come with me now. But when I am me again I'll go to his house, get you out – your body and this you – and kill him. My only chance is to leave without you."

Chapter twenty

"It felt like it at the time." Adam bristled at the Questioner's pompous tone.

The Questioner smiled. "Not to her." His hands shook as he pushed the Dictaphone back and forward across the table.

"I couldn't take Marion with me," Adam said. "And that brings me onto the ninth rule, the final one."

"Which is?"

"I nicked it from the Scouts," Adam said. "Be prepared for anything. It didn't quite go to plan."

Marion paced anxiously around the room in Williams' mind. Adam kept out of the way, knowing what was coming.

"How are 'you' going to kill him?" Marion emphasised 'you'.

"I have to work out the details," Adam admitted.

"You should've taken up karate," Marion said. "You could blow his house up. Or would that kill us conservatory kids too?"

Adam pictured the girls in the conservatory. He didn't say anything. Marion rounded on him.

"You're leaving Evie and Michelle?" she asked.

"I'll only have time to save you," Adam said softly. "A couple of seconds to get you back to your body before Williams notices you're gone from his head. If he skims off before I kill his body, he'll still be out there, taking other kids, or coming after us. I have to stop him."

"There must be another way," Marion said.

Marion clung to her brother fiercely. Her small hands dug into the centre of his back.

"It'll be alright," Adam said. He closed his eyes to her smeary tears and stretched through her arms, back into Hannah's connection and then, in a blur, slipped out through the keyhole.

He lay in the corridor, eyes shut. He hated leaving Marion but at least she was as annoying as normal – a good sign.

He crawled along the corridor to Hannah's door. It was wide open, not the way he'd left it. Hannah lay face down like a star fish, as if she'd been pushed to the floor. And stood over her – her eyes wide with innocence – was Marion.

"What have you done?" Adam asked. He bent over Hannah and prodded her cautiously. Imogen and Henry slept on.

"That won't work," Marion said guiltily. "She's out cold. I kept up my karate lessons."

"That's not possible," said Adam.

"I watched you go through the keyhole. I figured if you could do it, I could too. Didn't you notice me piggybacking on you?"

Adam hadn't noticed, but if Marion had hitched a lift like that, who else could?

"Well, that was stupid to knock Hannah out. Now I can't go anywhere," Adam said. "I'm tied to her, she's my connector."

"Cut her off."

Marion's solution was delivered bluntly. "I'll do it for you."

She ran to his back and, without warning, dug her hands deep into the black connection.

"Good effort," Adam hissed. "How about trying to wake her up? That might be more useful."

"Get off me," Adam cried twisting to look behind him. Hannah rolled over and moaned loudly.

"Nearly there," Marion said. She'd somehow divided Hannah's connection into seven ropes which she twisted one after the other. Each twist cut through the connection.

"That stings," Adam said. "Stop it!"

Marion twisted the last of the ropes. And then she gasped.

Light started dripping out of Adam's back. Leaking swathes of colour, streaming out like kite tails where Marion had severed the connection.

"I didn't mean to!" she said.

Adam looked at the colours drifting around him. He ran his fingers through the lights, wondering what was going on and why Marion was shouting, 'Sorry! Sorry! Sorry!' behind his back. But it was all very pretty.

And there was the girl, Hannah, on the floor, she had lights too. Hers were twinkling, but fading one by one until they all disappeared. Adam watched, struggling to form thoughts.

"It doesn't matter," Adam slurred.

"Yes it does."

Marion forced her hands deep into Adam's back and plaited the remains of the connection. She intuitively shoved them back in, a glorious bundle. Adam staggered forward as he was hit by his own personality reforming. He breathed deeply, settling into his skimming body.

"I think I need to sit down," he said.

"We don't have time," Marion replied. "Hannah'll wake up soon. Go on, do your skimming thing."

"Because of your little stunt we're both stuck in Williams' head. I can't go anywhere until I know where Williams' body is in reality..."

"Well then, let's go and find out." said Marion.

Adam shrugged. Did he have any other options?

Leaving the three Williams children sleeping, they crept along the corridor stumbling in the darkness.

Marion tapped on Adam's back as he chose the passage that rose steeply. Her eyes were like two full moons in the darkness.

"As soon as Williams gets back into his head, from wherever he's skimmed to, he'll be looking for you. Come on, we have to move quickly and get out of here."

The corridor narrowed until it became so tight their bodies touched both velvety walls. Marion whispered constantly about Michelle and Evie. As they squeezed their way through the passageway Adam finally told her to shut up.

Abruptly it widened, and they found themselves in a dead space, a wilting yucca plant on a table opposite a door sign-posted: 'Emergency Exit.'

That was the only way forward.

A security bar straddled the door. Adam pushed down firmly

and it gave way. A crack appeared, allowing him a direct view into the epicentre of Williams' mind. Adam crept through the doorway with Marion following close behind.

It looked like a waiting room. Beige plastic chairs were set out in orderly rows, one after another, attached at their hips. Dull paintings hung at regular intervals on the light green walls. The floor was covered with a thick brown carpet. In front of a glass window was a reception desk, with a computer, some post-it notes and a suggestion box on it.

"I have a suggestion for this," Marion said sweeping the box onto the floor. She stamped on it furiously.

Adam sighed. None of this gave him the slightest clue where Williams was in the real world.

Ignoring his sister, he peered at the computer screen. It was dead. He pulled open the drawers and rifled through them, while Marion examined the doors which led from the waiting room.

"Help me a bit?" Marion said, rattling a door handle.

Adam tossed her a bunch of keys he'd found at the bottom of the drawer, and went back to the computer screen. This was surely his ticket out, as soon as it sprang into life, he could place himself and then he and Marion would be gone. His fingers teased the keyboard.

"Back in a moment," Marion said.

Adam turned to stop her, but it was too late. She'd disappeared through one of the doors. He scrambled over the chair, but by the time he got to the door she was coming back through it, smiling broadly.

"I knew they'd be here somewhere," she said smugly. "So now you don't have to leave them."

Adam stared at Marion in disbelief as Michelle and Evie followed her through the door and stood looking around the waiting room, blinking rapidly.

Evie gripped Michelle's hand tightly.

"I don't like this," she said and began to cry.

"Don't worry," Marion said. "You'll be home soon."

She walked across to Adam. "Okay, let's go."

Adam looked at her in horror over the computer screen.

"Go?" he whispered. "I told you Marion, I can't. It's not that easy. Until this comes on, I don't know where I am."

"I do," said a soft voice. It was Hannah.

She strode out from behind the door Adam and Marion had come through. "But none of you are going anywhere. Adam, we had an agreement."

Hannah addressed the huddled girls: "I'm sorry but you three don't feature in it. Sit down and shut up."

Michelle and Evie sat down immediately. Marion assumed her karate pose. Hannah just laughed.

"Nothing's changed," she said to Adam. "Get these three back to where my dad left them and we'll be fine."

"I'm not going back," said Marion. "You can't make me!"

"Adam?" Hannah asked as if expecting him to deal with his wayward sister.

"Come here now," Adam said, "all of you." He beckoned to Michelle and Evie, who rose shakily and made their way towards the desk.

Marion's fist thumped into the computer. The waiting room walls flared with static energy, as the screen flickered into life. Williams was in his conservatory.

"That looks like me, what's wrong with my body?" Evie asked anxiously, looking at her gaunt figure on the computer over Adam's shoulder.

"You better do something," Marion said to Adam.

"Too late, dad's on his way," laughed Hannah. She lunged towards the desk and grabbed at Michelle, who ducked down out of her reach.

"He'll be here any second, you're all staying."

"Adam!" Marion said crossly, "NOW!"

Adam gripped Marion's wrists tightly. Time, place, energy. It was the quickest that he'd ever placed himself but would it be fast enough? Williams would be coming after them. There was no way of stopping him. It was time to find out if he had the strength to pull these girls to safety.

A glimmer of light. Adam skimmed through a stranger looking at Williams' manicured garden. A neighbour looking out of a window, someone pulling up in a car. He moved in circles searching for a way out.

Marion shouted something behind him. Adam glanced backwards. Hannah was clinging onto Michelle's waist, hair blowing across her grinning face.

Adam heard her shouts, they mingled with Michelle's yelps of fear.

Williams was there – he had Hannah's leg – pulling her backwards, using her body to leverage himself forward.

Adam's body rippled with exertion. He was skimming himself and five passengers through a string of hosts. It would have been impressive, if there wasn't so much screaming.

Now Williams had reached Michelle, she was crying out in pain. He climbed her like a ladder, booting Hannah in the face. She tumbled into the darkness, her arms outstretched. Hannah's fingers grasped in desperation, trying to get a purchase on anything but she fell back into the gleam of light.

Evie screamed. Williams had anchored his fist deep into her hair and was using his other to punch Marion in the stomach. As he clambered over Marion's squirming body, she kicked and bit furiously, but there was nothing she could do without letting go of her brother or Evie.

Adam's heart beat furiously. As every second passed, Williams was hurting the girls, they couldn't cling on for much longer. He had to stop and protect them. There! Someone familiar. What was she doing here? He dragged the girls into the stadium, onto his mother's empty stage.

"Is this Mum's head?" Marion asked in confusion.

"Yes, RUN!" replied Adam.

The stadium's spotlights blazed into life as the girls ran for cover in the wings. Williams stood opposite Adam, panting heavily. He smiled slowly and then drew his right fist back and smashed Adam in the face. Adam's head rocked backwards, his shoulders followed, but he took a step and regained his balance. The screen at the back of the stage flickered on.

In reality Adam's mum was running. Her heart beat through the speakers, like a metronome for Williams' punches.

Williams punched furiously as Adam raised his hands to protect his face. Williams hit him again and again. The blows rained down. Adam staggered to his knees on the slippery stage. He blinked blood, trying to see where Marion was but instead he saw a version of his mother, sitting blankly in the front row. Adam reached his hand out to her, and croaked her name. Williams stamped down on Adam's fingers and ground his heel into the boy's palm.

Adam put his head down. Whatever strength he had left was stolen by his mother's indifference. He was spent.

Satisfied that Adam was beaten, Williams walked to the wings of the stage to retrieve 'his' girls. They skittered away, running rings around him. Williams lunged for Marion, she ran straight towards Adam.

"Get up you idiot! This isn't complicated skimming stuff," Marion shrieked. "Help me!"

She jumped over his legs with Williams seconds behind her.

Adam raised his foot. It was enough. Williams was sent sprawling onto the stage.

Marion crouched and took Adam's head into her hands to

protect it, as Williams scrambled to his feet. He walked back towards them, rubbing his chin where it'd hit the stage.

"You're coming with me," he said.

Adam stared as Williams came closer.

"I'm sorry Adam," Marion said, "I don't know what to do." She wiped her nose with the back of her hand.

"It's me who's sorry," Adam replied. "I started this, but I can't end it."

Williams stopped millimetres from Adam's nose.

"Get up!" he ordered. But his voice was drowned out by the speakers. Rusted feedback slit the air.

"Marion! Marion! Marion!"

Marion covered her ears against the sound of her name, repeated over and over by her desperate mother.

Williams' eyes locked onto what was appearing on the screen behind the children. It was showing the reality that Adam's mother could see. Adam watched as it blinked on and off, but was steady enough to make out Williams' conservatory and the girls slumped in it, tied to their abductor with green ribbon. No wonder his mum was screaming.

Adam grabbed Marion's hand on the stage and pointed to the screen. Someone was pulling their mum backwards. From this angle it looked like Spod. The detective smashed down the conservatory door. Two policewomen pushed their way through.

"Do I really look that bad?" Marion asked critically, squinting at the screen as their mum shook her unresponsive body in the conservatory and wailed: "What's wrong with her?"

Swarming paramedics pushed her aside as they slapped oxygen masks over the girls' faces.

"It's okay," Spod was saying on the screen to Adam's mum, words of comfort denying her terrified face. And then Williams eyes opened in the conservatory, he had gone back to his body.

"I want to get back now," Marion shouted over the stadium's speakers. "I want my mum!"

Chapter twenty-one

Adam didn't hang around to watch the girls wake up in the conservatory. He was in no mood to witness his mother's smothering reunion with Marion.

Soon he'd head back to his real body, which was lying on the floor of Spod's bedroom. But first he had to take care of a few things. Like Williams. The police had handcuffed him and were leading him away to a waiting car. But that wouldn't stop him from skimming and Adam knew who would be getting a visit: him, Marion, and Spod. Hannah had been right all along, Williams had to be taken care of. He had to go back into Williams' mind.

"It's too late," Hannah said. "Listen, can you hear any buzzing?" Adam shook his head, he didn't.

"That's because dad's gone. Oh, but wait," she smiled and flicked her hair. "I'm sure he'll come back to see you."

She stood up and walked to the reception desk.

"I'll let him know you're here."

Hannah put her hands out to the computer screen, Adam was beside her in seconds, holding her wrists.

"Don't do this," he said. "I can help you."

"How?" Hannah asked. "All you had to do was kill dad. But oh no, look what you did. You saved all the little girls, let dad escape and now he's off finding more bodies. We'll be moved into them later. This time he isn't even having the decency to kidnap them. How can you help us?"

"I'm taking you away to hide you," said Adam.

"I like hide and seek," Henry interrupted.

"I suppose it's worth a try," Hannah sighed. "I don't want a new body."

"I do," Henry said, hopping up and down. "I hope its a boy this time. That'd be great."

Hannah raised her eyebrows.

"It's definitely time to go," she said.

The Williams children gripped their hands together. Adam held Hannah's hands tightly; he looked deeply into her eyes.

"Ready?" he asked. He shut his eyes and they were gone.

Adam returned alone to the empty beige waiting room of Williams' mind. The man was capable of anything. He had to stop him for good.

Williams' computer flickered, the detective was driving the police car. It was time for Adam to visit his familiar tendrils.

Adam skimmed. The detective had one eye on the round-about ahead, and a lorry which was changing lanes, and one eye on Williams in the back seat of the car.

Adam skimmed. The lorry driver was singing.

Adam didn't hesitate. He forced the driver's hand to swing the wheel, his foot to stamp on the accelerator, his other hand to yank on the handbrake.

In the split second it took to topple the lorry, Adam was in Williams' head, smashing the computer that would bring Williams back. Then he skimmed into the detective, grabbing his tendrils, forcing him to look up and see the dark shadow of the lorry crashing down on him. There was a tiny moment to accelerate furiously, a hair's whisper for the front of the car to escape the final crushing momentum of the lorry – but not the back.

Adam awoke in Spod's room.

He'd killed Williams.

Just like that.

Chapter twenty two

A<small>DAM WAITED IN</small> S<small>POD'S BEDROOM FOR A WHILE, HOPING THAT SHE</small> <small>WOULD RETURN, BUT</small> S<small>HE DIDN'T.</small> He guessed that she'd have some explaining to do. She must have taken the police to Williams house and come up with a plausible tale. Adam stumbled down the stairs, he couldn't stay at Spod's forever, but the thought of going home to his parents was unappealing.

"Where are they?" The Questioner's voice carried the same sound as a snake slithering across a tiled floor, dry.

Adam raised his head and looked at the man's jowly face, his tired skin, the twitches that scurried across his face as if he couldn't quite control the body he was in.

"Tell me where my children are."

Adam's mouth opened in surprise.

"You're...Williams!!" he gasped.

Adam pushed away from the table and edged back towards the door, as Williams lunged for him over the table, knocking the Dictaphone onto the floor.

"Get off me!" Adam yelled, as the older man rounded the table and grabbed his hoodie.

Adam kicked furiously at Williams' legs in vain. Flabby as he was, Williams' punch to Adam's stomach floored him. He stood over Adam, staring down at him.

Williams stepped back and glowered at Adam's crumpled figure. Adam skated his fingers across the floor wishing he had something to defend himself with.

"For the first time today, I believe you," the man said.

"Is that why I'm here? It's not to help me, it's so you can get your children back! And whose body have you stolen now?" Adam demanded.

"Someone unimportant," Williams said. He tried to squat down in front of Adam but it was more like collapsing. As he hit the ground a gush of wind blew thick dust across the floor.

"I found this body in the river when you crushed my old one under the lorry. I skimmed into this carcass and now I can't get out. I'm the only life left in it and the suction's phenomenal. There's a tenth rule for you..."

Adam shuffled along the wall, away from the man. Williams tried to follow him around the room, his legs crab-like as he jerked sideways across the floor.

"I'd hoped that your 'rules' would tell me something useful that would get me out of this pickle. But alas, no."

"You're supposed to be dead," Adam said.

"My body is, but not my mind," Williams sneered. "You owe me. Take me to the Board. They'll love this, 'full possession' of someone for such a long time has never been done before. The research stopped after my wife, well, you know what happened to her." He wiped spittle away from his chin.

"I don't want anything to do with you." Adam whispered.

"We're very alike Adam, you and me."

"No we're not."

146

"Yes we are," Williams said. "Every word's on tape. We're both killers. We're both extraordinary skimmers. And we both have family difficulties. Help me and I'll help you. I can give you parents who love you. Put you in a new body, into a baby."

"Wouldn't you like that? To be the one that mummy loves the most? You've cried about it, now's your chance to make it happen. You and me Adam, against the world."

"What about your own kids?" Adam asked, appalled.

"Get me out of this body," Williams said. "And then I'll worry about them. You need to help me. Your tenth rule should be 'avoid the dying.' I haven't got long left in this body before I'll be sucked into oblivion."

Adam swallowed hard. His plan to hide the Williams kids from their father was so simple. And now, looking at the man in front of him, it seemed so absolutely stupid.

"I have to go," Adam said. He shut his eyes against the leering smile of Williams, who was crawling towards him, placed himself, and skimmed through a couple of nurses in the hospital to his grandad's head, full of memories – and the Williams children taking shelter within them.

Hannah stood in the doorway of the farmhouse, a blanket across her shoulders to keep warm. Henry and Imogen sheltered in her arms. Banks of clouds sprinted before a cool breeze which brought sharp drizzle on its edges.

The children stared upwards as lightning in greens, yellows and purples criss-crossed the sky, highlighting the weathervane. Waves of thunder rolled down the hillsides buffeting their bodies. Hannah laughed wildly at the sky.

"You can't stay here," Adam yelled. "My grandad's dying. His memories are collapsing."

"We guessed," Hannah said, "It's awesome to watch though isn't it? Look at that!"

Adam looked to where she was pointing. Jagged lightning attacked the sky and split it in two. The ground shook with anticipated glee and squirmed with pleasure at the torrential rain which the clouds were unleashing.

"We've been waiting for this," Hannah said. She pointed at the tear.

"You're insane!" Adam yelled. "You don't know where that goes!" His voice got lost in the wind that plummeted up and down. He grabbed onto the corner of the farmhouse to steady himself. The ground started to split, cracking up the hill, mirroring the sky.

"Come with us," Hannah called. The blanket blew from her shoulders. She grasped Henry and Imogen by the arms firmly leading them forward.

"No!" Adam yelled. "Don't do it Hannah," but she was already on the edge of the crack, fighting to keep her balance as her hair whipped around her. She stopped and turned to face Adam.

"It's all right, honestly." she said. "Look, you can see, it leads on..." But her words disappeared. Adam strained to hear, she was beckoning him forward, pointing into the hole. He tightened his grip on the wall. There was no way he was letting go.

"It's so pretty," Imogen's voice called as she stepped into the ground. Henry followed.

Hannah pointed to the sky and saluted as it folded back on itself, peeling from the inside out, bruised reds sparkling through the rain drops. Grandad was at the end.

As Adam opened his eyes in the hospital basement Williams moved back, pulling his hand guiltily away. Adam felt a sticky sheen on his forehead; had that come from the man's palm?

"Where did you go?" Williams' lips sagged around the words. He was struggling to breathe, let alone speak. The body he inhabited was sweating profusely. A red flush swam through its skin. Starting at the nose where it was light pink, it spread out to an angry magenta at the tips of the fingers.

Adam put his head back against the wall. It was so easy to refuse the man. To watch as Mr Williams' life drained out the body. To feel the sweet knowledge that Adam was safe. Marion was safe. And of course Spod. They all would be safe. To know that Williams wouldn't steal any more children and even better, that Adam didn't have to kill him, again.

Williams looked at his hands, trying to get them to move. His eyes were lit with fanatical desire, but he was collapsing internally, shrivelling before Adam's eyes in an unresponsive body. Finally with extreme concentration Williams managed to move one finger toward Adam.

"I understand," he slurred. "I'd do the same."

Adam swore profusely at the dying body. He wasn't the same as this man!

"I will regret this," he said, "but apparently today is the day for new beginnings."

Pulling his sleeves down over his hands, he moved nearer to the body and took Williams's slick palms into his.

They stood together on Adam's dark plain. Williams, in a shrunken form, hung weakly from Adam's shoulder.

"I knew you'd see sense," Williams said.

Two figures were advancing from the distance. It was the same pair as before – the Board were paying a visit.

"You're late," the woman said. She looked Adam up and down piercingly. "What happened with your sister?" she asked.

"I got Marion back," said Adam. "Williams was doing a little research with her and a couple more girls."

"It was an experiment in full possession..." Williams began, and then his mouth fell open in horror.

"No!" he cried, "you can't!"

Adam closed his eyes to Williams' desperation. When he opened them again, he was alone.

Chapter twenty three

Williams' body lay spread-eagled on the floor. It was already giving off a sickeningly sweet odour. Whoever had owned it originally was long gone, and now Williams was gone too.

Adam pushed the body away and wiped his prints off every thing using the sleeves of his hoodie. He held his nose as he rooted around in the body's pockets, looking for the door key.

Adam unlocked the door and made his way as fast as possible through the hospital basement.

He took a lift up to the ward where his grandfather lay lifeless. A nurse put her fingers to her lips and shook her head. She pointed to the closed curtain around the bed.

Marion and Adam's parents stood solemnly by grandad's body, their heads bowed.

"Hey," Adam said softly.

Marion looked up.

"Mum bought me a mobile," she whispered triumphantly. waving her prize in Adam's direction.

"Good for you," Adam said.

"I called Spod, I thought you'd turn up here eventually. She's on her way."

"Shush," his mother said. "Show some respect for the dead."

Adam backed out and made his way down the hot ward. At least Spod would be pleased to see him, wouldn't she?

He sat on a chair next to the lifts and waited anxiously. Why was he so nervous? His palms itched with confusion. The lift doors sighed and opened, it wasn't Spod. And neither were the next three visitors to the ward. His fingers drummed on his thigh.

Adam picked up a magazine from the table next to him and thumbed through it trying to distract himself. Someone had already filled in all of the crosswords and puzzles. He flicked through some articles on hairstyles and plastic surgery. And then she was there.

"Thinking of changing your hair?" she laughed.

"No!" snapped Adam.

Spod sat down beside him on a chair, and put her hand onto his arm. Adam shrugged her off embarrassed by the magazine.

"What happened?" he asked. "You left me with Hannah – you were supposed to look after me!"

Spod leaned back and shut her eyes.

"You can't even ask how I am?" she sighed.

"Are you all right?" Adam said automatically.

Why was he being such a fool? This was Spod, Spod of all people.

"I was cut off," Spod said, "I didn't leave you. I tried to find you again, but I couldn't. So I called your mum, and the police and took them to Williams' house. Are you mad at me?"

"No," Adam said wishing that she'd put her hand back on his arm. Why had he pushed her away?

"I've blown any chance of getting a Board license now," Spod sighed.

"Sorry," Adam said softly. "I couldn't have done any of it without you."

He finally put his hand out to catch hers, but Spod was up on her feet, waving to Marion who'd appeared with her new phone. Adam squeezed his empty fingers shut and stood up next to her. Spod turned to face him anxiously.

Epilogue

THE DETECTIVE SHRUGGED HIS COAT OFF AND PASSED IT TO THE NERVOUS CARETAKER STANDING NEXT TO HIM. Rubbing his eyes wearily, he pushed the basement door open. On the floor lay the shabbily dressed body of a middle-aged man. Coughing at the fetid smell, the detective bent down to get a closer look. Then he spied something under the table.

Also from Mogzilla:

HAYWIRED
By Alex Keller

In the quiet village of Little Wainesford, Ludwig von Guggenstein is about to have his unusual existence turned inside out. When he and his father are blamed for a fatal accident during the harvest, a monstrous family secret is revealed. Soon Ludwig will begin to uncover diabolical plans that span countries and generations while ghoulish machines hunt him down. He must fight for survival, in a world gone haywire.

ISBN: 978-1-906132-33-0
UK: £7.99

http://www.mogzilla.co.uk/haywired

LONDON DEEP

By Robin Price & Paul McGrory

Jemima Mallard is having a bad day. First she loses her air, then someone steals her houseboat, and now the Youth Cops think she's mixed up with a criminal called Father Thames. Not even her dad, a Chief Inspector with the 'Dult Police, can help her out this time. Oh – and London's still sinking. It's been underwater ever since the climate upgrade. All in all, it's looking like deep trouble.

ISBN: 978-1-906132-03-3

Chosen as a 'Recommended Read' for World Book Day 2011. One of the *Manchester Book Award's* 24 recommended titles for. 2010.

'This is a terrifically atmospheric page-turning adventure told with words and comic art... it's a rattling good read and one in which you are sure to be drawn into Jemima's exploits of survival.' – *Lovereading.co.uk*

FATHER THAMES

Rebellious teen Jemima Mallard has done the unthinkable. She's joined the Youth Police Department (YPD).

Is she serious, or is she spying for the criminal Father Thames? Fellow YPD officer Nick Mallard isn't sure. Before he can test her loyalty, the two must go to war.

Their city is under attack. From the Thames Barrier Reef to the Sink estates, strange ships have breached the defences. London hasn't seen anything like these raiders – adults and kids sailing and working together. But orders are orders, Jem must find find a way to stop them.

ISBN: 9781906132040
Price: £7.99